An Adventurer's Heart

Book 2 of Adventures on Brad

by

Tao Wong

Copyright

This is a work of fiction. Names, characters, businesses, places, events and incidents are either the products of the author's imagination or used in a fictitious manner. Any resemblance to actual persons, living or dead, or actual events is purely coincidental.

This book is licensed for your personal enjoyment only. This book may not be re-sold or given away to other people. If you would like to share this book with another person, please purchase an additional copy for each recipient. If you're reading this book and did not purchase it, or it was not purchased for your use only, then please return to your favorite book retailer and purchase your own copy. Thank you for respecting the hard work of this author.

Books in the
Adventures on Brad series

A Healer's Gift
An Adventurer's Heart
A Dungeon's Soul
The Arena's Call
The Adventurer's Bond
The Forest's Silence

Contents

Chapter 1

As the sun begins to set, a pair of Adventurers approach the Northern city gates of Karlak. The small dungeon town is bisected by a river, overlooked by rolling hills, and surrounded by wooden walls. The town radiates outwards from its chief income source, a Beginner Dungeon with buildings closest to the Dungeon and the town center made of stone, and those further away with cheaper materials such as wood and clay. As the pair near the walls, the Guards relax as the pair are well known, and their presence barely missed. After all, these two Adventurers had left only two days ago.

The taller of the pair is only five-foot-eight, a friendly smile gracing his face as he nods to the guards. The friendly Adventurer is broad and stocky, his muscular frame currently burdened by a large bag slung over his shoulder. The second of the two is a shorter Catkin female, black fur and bestial, cat features on a slim build. She is dressed in a jerkin and shirt, with a dirty, once dark-blue coat trailing behind her. A brace of throwing daggers lie across her torso, another larger pair rest on her hips as she glides alongside her partner.

"Matthew, Jason!" the human Adventurer calls out, waving in greeting as he shifts the bag behind him again.

"Daniel, Asin. A successful trip I take it?" The two guards grin, glancing at the bag and the roll of dark fur that lies strapped to the top of it.

"Yes!" Daniel answers them, pride radiating in his voice.

"Well, best get in. We'll be closing the gates soon." The two guards beckon the Adventurers into the town, and Daniel nods in thanks. Asin chuffs a greeting as well, the guards flashing a quick, narrowed eye once-over at the Beastkin before stepping aside.

When the pair is a distance away, Asin moves closer to her friend, grating out in a low purr, "They like you. The guards."

Daniel nods, smiling slightly as he rubs his nose as it attempts to get used to the unwashed, rotting stink of the city, "Yeah. They're a decent lot mostly."

Asin chuffs again, shaking her head at Daniel but failing to contradict him directly. His experience and hers differed greatly as the Beastkin were an unwanted, barely tolerated minority in Brad still. If she had arrived alone, Asin knew she'd have to pay the toll for coming in and would have been hassled for leaving, even though she was a registered Adventurer like him. Daniel, however, had managed to build a good reputation in the town – his work in the Clinic as a free healer and his time spent socializing with the guards stood him in good stead. His presence shielded her and those with him, even if he himself never realized it.

The pair head deeper into the town, bypassing alleys that would take them into the various shopping districts and head directly to the Adventurer's Guild. The Guild is one of the few buildings in town able to afford the mana stones required to light the building all night long and does so, staying open all hours of the day and night. They could afford this as the Guild was the exclusive purchaser of mana stones from the Adventurers who ventured into the Dungeon, their monopoly guaranteed by Kingdom law. It is also at the Guild that the two expect to turn in their successful quest.

It is no surprise to either of the Adventurers to find that Liev, the red-haired senior Guild attendant, is still on duty. He rarely leaves the building and is often seen working the busy shifts late into the night when Adventurers returned from their Dungeon exploration. When the pair step into the building, Liev smiles as he spots them, straightening up for a moment from his usual slouched posture before the usual impassive demeanor returns.

"Asin, Daniel. Back already?" he says to them when the duo finally reach his window.

"Yes!" Daniel unslings his bag and unties the skin, dropping it on the counter as proof of their successful hunt.

A brief check is all that Liev requires to confirm the kill, and then he hands over their reward, a staggering 75 silver, and their deposit. A single silver could let a day laborer who skimped eat for a year, so the sum they have just earned still makes both Asin and Daniel grin. After all, it has only been a bare nine months since they first started Adventuring. The enormous sum for the Quest was due to the continued failures by other

Adventurers to complete the quest. As was custom, the city raised the bounty after each failure, using a portion of the failed Adventurers lost deposit to pay for the increase.

A brief moment later and both Adventurers receive a notification, the glowing black lines floating in their sight before disappearing.

Quest Complete!
+5,000 XP

The pair of Adventurers quickly take their piles of coin, thanking Liev before exiting to run their next errand. Asin leads Daniel to a butcher shop, having organized the additional trade to supplement their income. Shadow Cat meat was a rare treat and would be highly sought after by certain clientele, and the butcher had agreed to pay very well. Once again, Asin chuffs in pleasure at the thought of the coin they are about to earn and the fact that her party member had done most of the hard work carrying the meat back to town. In truth, while the work had been hard, Daniel knew the additional funds would help in paying off their accumulated debts.

Absently, Asin strokes the matching enchanted bracers on her arms. While they had greatly aided the pair in their battles, enchanted weaponry was extremely expensive and had driven both of them deeply into debt. Even now, with their recent windfall, they would have been unable to pay for the bracers if Tharuk, the enchanter, had not generously agreed to allow them to pay what they could, when they could. For Asin though, owing anyone, especially a Dwarf, was not something that sat well with her.

Meat deposited and payment received, the two Adventurers part ways. Asin to meet her family and Daniel to head to the Spinning Top, the inn where he resides. At the inn, Daniel greets Elise the innkeeper and owner before asking for food to be brought to his room, taking the time to wash himself down in the provided washbasin. After dinner, exhausted from a hard day's work, Daniel lies back on the clean sheets and falls asleep, completely forgetting about the dinner he had ordered.

***

As he sleeps, his enchanted ring of experience begins to draw forth the stored memories from its stone, replaying them through his mind and body in flashes. It is a strange experience as the memories and experiences that flow through his mind are always somewhat scattered.

In the morning, Asin is cooking breakfast, spreading herbs on the omelet and working the pan with little flicks of her hand. Mushrooms, field onions and more.

"Ugh, no mushrooms!" Daniel complains and Asin sniffs, ignoring his constant complaints about the delectable fungus. "I'll cook mine!"

Daniel takes over when Asin is done. Borrowing the pan, he cracks the eggs with professional ease. Instead of borrowing from her herbs though, he pulls his own out from his pack, separating each pouch and adding in the herbs with practiced flicks. Asin sniffs as she watches, though an eyebrow arches at his last addition.

"Papricha," Asin grates out.

"Yes, paprika. Love it," Daniel smirks and finishes up, tossing the omelet onto his plate and pulling out some bread to toast as well. "Want some?"

Asin pauses, nose wrinkling and whiskers trembling in the still air before she bobs her head, tail lazily waving behind her.

The Shadow Cat is crouched above Daniel, snarling at the downed Adventurer. He groans, pushing against the monster but it's already jumping away as Daniel tries to lever the monster off him, blood pooling on the ground from the cat's attack. A knife catches the Shadow Cat as it jumps away, Asin's Piercing Shot drilling into the creature's body, the knife twisting as it rotates in. Attached to the knife is a long iron chain, the end of which is wrapped around Asin's torso.

The creature's jump pulls the chain taut, jerking it to a stop and forcing the monster to fall with an ungainly crash. Asin, who is lighter, is pulled off her feet and falls on her behind. The snarls of pain and dismay from the pair of cats sound eerily similar to Daniel as he struggles to his feet.

Standing, Daniel jumps at the monster, slamming the mace down with his full strength onto the cat's prone form. He clips the creature's back leg, bruising and tearing muscle as the cat attempts to stand again. Asin rolls over, gripping the chain and yanking hard to throw the cat off balance and keeping it out of the shadows.

Daniel swings again, the blow catching the cat on its forehead, dazing the creature and then he kicks it away from the nearest shadows to the middle of the path they walk on. As he does, the knife finally dislodges, and Asin stumbles from the sudden release. She catches herself quickly enough to pull another knife to throw at the cat, even as the monster gets back onto its feet in another attempt to flee.

Walking back to the city, back bowed as he carries the quartered meat. Daniel asks, "Where did you learn to skin and butcher like that?"

"Father. Traditional," Asin chuffs, waving a hand around and then goes back to cleaning her claws, working to remove the accumulated blood and filth.

"Ah," Daniel nods slightly, a wry twist of the lips crossing his face. He never knew his father, a casualty of the mines a few years after he was born. His mother had died in childbirth, leaving him to grow up with his grandfather. Strange how that still stung, even after all these years.

Morning. The bells wake Daniel up and he pulls himself from the covers, drenched in sweat once again. He sighs, shaking his head at the memories and unpleasant experiences he has gone through. Sometimes, it seemed that the minor gains in experience he received from the stones were not worth the hassle.

Chapter 2

"Ogres, ogres, ogres. Come out!" Daniel calls mockingly, swinging his mace around as he walks around the massive cavern that makes up the entrance to the seventh floor of the Dungeon in Karlak. Glow stones in the ceiling were so bright that lush grass and small trees grew in the cavern, a massive change from the cramped, cave-like floors above.

Asin's tail waves lazily in amusement, loping alongside Daniel as they search. His noisy entrance brings not one but two Ogres to them, and she shoots an annoyed glare at her companion. The creatures are on the smaller side, barely twelve feet tall, clad in their traditional loincloth and rags and each carries a crude wooden club in hand. Small or not, Asin would have preferred to start the day a little lighter. On spotting the intruders, the Ogres roar, charging the pair.

Bounding ahead, Asin slides a pair of throwing knives from her bandolier, targeting the lead Ogre's right eye with one knife. It roars, raising a hand to block the knife, and is now unable to see the follow-up throw charged with Piercing Shot slice through the air into its chest and lung. Angered at being tricked, and in pain, the Ogre dashes forward to smite the smaller Adventurer, but Asin skips back with ease. As she does, she throws another pair of knives underhanded, the Ogre is so close this time that lightning from Asin's charged aura also strikes the monster.

By her side, Daniel rushes Asin's opponent, using his shield to ram the monster and forcing it back further still with a Shield Bash. The Ogre stumbles, catching its balance and Daniel lashes out once quickly at its knee, cracking his mace against it before stepping back so as not to be surrounded as the second Ogre finally arrives.

As the uninjured Ogre attacks Daniel, he backpedals to the side and puts the other Ogre in the way, forcing his second opponent to pull back on its attack. Staying close behind Daniel, Asin does the same, pelting the first Ogre with a knife each time it tries to move its hand away from its face. Asin moves smoothly, pulling extra knives from her satchel and passing it to her primary hand when she can. Unable to properly see what it is doing, it swings its club wildly, allowing Daniel to duck beneath and attack its knee, smashing again and again into the bruised limb until it cracks and gives way.

Once the first Ogre is immobilized, the two Adventurers turn their attention to the second Ogre. Their time with the Army has given them new ideas, new concepts to play with, and they put these ideas to work immediately. Instead of holding back and providing fire support, Asin rushes forward to join the fight with the Ogre directly. The second Ogre is forced to deal with two opponents, one on on either side, Daniel taking the side with the club and shedding any attacks the creature swings while Asin slices into its body with her long knives, dodging and cutting at the monster's flailing fist whenever it comes close.

As the Ogre swings an overhand blow, Daniel steps to the side swiftly and lashes out twice at the exposed arm, cracking the thumb bone that holds the club and forcing the Ogre to release it. Even as it deals with that pain, Asin ducks in and plunges her knives into its liver, dropping the monster to its knees before it collapses for the final time. Without pause, the Adventurers move towards the second Ogre whose attempt at crawling to them has been too slow. Dispatching it is done swiftly, Daniel shattering an elbow to allow Asin to plunge her knife into the back of its head. As the creature finally dies, it breaks apart in motes of blue light, leaving behind the mana crystal it was made from.

Asin lets out a little meow of happiness, dancing forwards to collect and verify the crystals. The monsters were created from mana by the goddess Erlis in Dungeons to remove the taint her nemesis Ba'al continually introduces into the mana flows of the world. It is the job of Adventurers to travel into Dungeons, defeating the monsters to help purge the taint and, of course, earn a living selling the mana crystals to the Guild. These mana crystals are then used for a wide variety of purposes, such as providing lighting sources, magical ingredients for powerful spells and even fertilizer for farms.

"Just three more floors to go, Asin," Daniel grins, rotating the mace around his hand in idle thought as they make their way to the next cavern. "Then we'll be done here."

Asin nods, nimbly skipping along in front of her companion and scanning the ground for potential traps. As they near the exit, she throws a hand up, and Daniel stops, waiting as she stares at the ground further. After a moment, she digs out her knife, moving to lightly score the earth which gives way with ease, revealing a crude pit trap covered with sod and grass. Standing and eyeing the trap, she leads Daniel around it, neither bothering to set the trap off. The dungeon would recreate it soon enough if they did.

"Dungeon Boss, hard," Asin points out, and Daniel grimaces, nodding in agreement. "New skills."

"True. We'll need more skills for sure. Still, we're learning to fight together quite well," Daniel points out as he waits for her to clear the passageway.

Asin just chuffs in agreement, nimbly moving along the smaller passageway that connects to the next cavern. They certainly seem to have learned to handle two Ogres quite well. Perhaps their time with the Army, listening to conversations and observing the fighting, had not been a total waste.

***

"Evening, Asin, Daniel. Seventh floor?" Liev asks, sorting through the mana stones with practiced ease and drawing his conclusion from their quality and quantity. Asin nods, chuffing in agreement, eyes tracking the motion of his hands with deep intensity. "You really should get better armor if you are working that floor you know, both of you."

"I wish!" Daniel mutters shaking his head. "I still owe Tharuk another gold for the bracers, and then I've had to save up for the armor itself!"

"Mmm… and you buy from Maxwell, right?" Liev asks, and Daniel nods. "And you, Asin?"

Asin shrugs, waggling her hands sideways a bit, black fur licked clean from their romp.

"Ah, no loyalty. Not surprising I guess, most armorers don't really build for Catkin." Liev finishes his calculations and pushes the document forward to show them how much they earned today. Daniel reads the document over, announcing the total for Asin who nods in agreement. They quickly split the earnings, sliding the coins into their pouches as Liev smiles slightly. "Well, I'd check the Quest Board then. I believe Maxwell posted a job there recently."

"Thanks, Liev!" Hurrying over, Daniel and Asin scan the board before finally finding the one Liev spoke of.

Quest: An Armorer's Masterpiece

This is a multi-stage quest that will require a flexible and dedicated team to finish. Interested parties should speak with Maxwell the Armorer directly.

Rewards: 1 full set of iron armor upon completion of the Quest chain.

"Ooooh…" Daniel stares, salivating at the thought of a full set of iron armor. The cost of his Leather Armor was staggering, especially for one who until recently was just a Miner. The idea of a quest chain that would gain him a full set made him crack a wide smile. Then he stops, realizing it is only a single set. He looks over to Asin, who looks at it and makes a face too.

"Only one," Asin growls, scratching at her ear.

"Yeah, I guess this won't work," Daniel sighs, shaking his head. No wonder other groups hadn't jumped on it yet. Working out who got the set would be troublesome especially since most groups were larger than their pair.

"Split. Me three-quarters," Asin points to herself and then points to the quest.

"What? No, that won't work. We aren't even the same size!" Daniel protests and her tail whips around in annoyance.

"No. Dungeon earnings. Three-quarters." Asin points to herself again, hoping he gets it.

"Oh…" Daniel nods slowly, then realizes something. "For how long?"

"Paid off. Then half." Asin shrugs and Daniel nods, doing the math in his head. At their current earnings, that would be at least another half-year, if not year. Dungeon delving on the seventh floor was good money, but not that good. Though perhaps if they went deeper, they might earn more too.

Having finished his calculations, Daniel nods and pulls down the quest marker, flashing Asin a grateful smile. He walks over to Liev quickly, paying the refundable deposit that is required for the quest.Since it is a chain quest, the Guild have made it a refundable deposit so that Adventurers can back out of the quest once they receive full details from Maxwell. Thanking Liev, the two Adventurers make plans to visit Maxwell's shop the next morning when it opens. That done, Asin heads into the Beastkin's quarter, loping off at a steady pace while Daniel moves to visit the Clinic.

The Clinic, as it is known in Karlak, is in a poorer quarter of the city near the walls. Made of wood and clay, the Clinic spans two whole buildings with only a few rooms for outpatient treatment, with most of the other rooms filled with patients who require on-going care. A free institution run by Khy'ra and other volunteers, the building is always crowded with individuals who needed healing. After all, good medical care is both difficult to find and expensive, especially healing spells.

As Daniel enters, the townsfolk within wave, call out and nod in greeting to the young Adventurer. He smiles at them all, mentally checking his own Mana pool before he heads deeper, stopping only long enough to announce his presence to Khy'ra with a kiss and hug before he enters his room. It only takes a brief moment before he is joined by his first patient in the room who proceeds to ramble on even around his nasty cough.

Hours later, the Clinic doors are finally closed, and outpatients are forced to leave until the next day. Daniel groans, shaking his head as his Mana is entirely drained leaving him with a slight headache and tired muscles. Arms wrap around him, the comforting smell of his girlfriend tickling his nostrils. For a moment, Daniel wonders how even in the midst of a city, the buxom, blonde elf could smell of trees and wet earth, before he just revels in the hug. She squeezes him again, and then he turns around, seeking her lips.

"Hello there." Khy'ra laughs as she breaks away from the kiss, still holding on to him.

"Hello." He kisses her again hungrily, picking her up and depositing her on the wooden slab they use for an inspection bed.

"Ah, we're doing that, now are we?" she teases, not stopping him as his hands wander to the back of her dress.

"Yes!" he growls, and the older elf laughs again, helping him take it off. Young human males were always so energetic!

***

"Maxwell." Daniel greets the burly smith as he comes out from the back of his forge, wiping sweat from his forehead.

"Daniel. Asin." Maxwell nods in greeting, eyes automatically dropping to their weapons as he assesses them. "More repairs?"

"Actually, no. We're here about the quest." Daniel steps forward, proffering the sheet to show that they have been officially assigned the quest.

"Oh!" Maxwell deflates a little, eyeing the two of them. "Well, I guess…"

Asin's eyes narrow at the less than enthusiastic response and even Daniel seems a bit taken back. Seeing their reaction, Maxwell hastens to add, "It's nothing against you two. It's just, well, most people have turned me down after hearing the details."

"Well, you might as well tell us," Daniel points out, and Maxwell nods, though he pauses first to get some more water to wet his throat. It is only after he comes back with his own glass that he remembers to offer some to his guests who both hastily decline, impatient to hear about the quest.

"Right then. There are multiple parts to this quest, and once you start, I expect you to finish. I'll build your armor as we finish each portion though I won't make final adjustments until the end. That way, if you decide to quit, I can always sell it later on. And I'm not splitting the making of it – it gets made for only one person!" warns Maxwell and both Adventurers nod in agreement. When they decline to speak further, Maxwell huffs and continues. "Right, there are three parts to this, and you'll be traveling for at least two parts. It'll take you away from the Dungeon for at least three months."

Maxwell then stops, just waiting for the Adventurers to decline. Instead, the pair frown in unison before Daniel speaks up, "Ummm… Maybe you can explain what it is we'll be doing a bit more?"

"I am ready to work on my Masterpiece to get my Master's designation." Maxwell unconsciously reaches out and touches the silver chain behind his tunic. "However, I need specific materials for what I have in mind and most of it isn't available in this town. The things that I need are expensive, and none of the sellers are willing to guarantee my delivery. That's where you come in.

"The first part is getting the materials here. I've already made the purchases, but they're all waiting in Silverstone for pickup. Your job is to travel there and then safeguard my purchases on the next merchant caravan that comes back to Karlak," Maxwell continues.

"After that, I need you to bring a half-dozen grade B Type III mana stones. I need to power the forge for three days straight, and anything weaker than a grade B will not give us enough heat. If you can't get Type III, smaller Grade B stones will do, but you'll need to get more of them," Maxwell points out, eyeing the two. The last he'd heard, these two were only on the seventh floor which didn't give out grade III stones, even from the chest.

"Lastly, I need you to bring me three intact sacs of venom from the Querk Spiders that live in the Pearly Forests. Those need to be done last because the venom only lasts for a week and it'll take you at least two days to get back here. So, you still interested?"

Daniel and Asin look at one another and then Daniel asks hesitatingly, "So, Silverstone is the biggest trip, right? It's nearly three weeks journey from here. Can we work as guards or something on the way there? There's no time sensitivity to that portion, right?"

Maxwell harrumphs for a moment then shrugs, "No. I figured you Adventurers would time your journey there with one of the caravans.

I don't care how you get there, but when you come back, your first and most important role is to keep my goods safe."

Daniel looks to Asin who meets his gaze, inclining her head slightly. Daniel smiles and turns to Max, saying, "We accept then."

Maxwell grins and offers his hand, "Really? You sure?"

Daniel nods and shakes the smith's hand, smiling. "We're sure. We'll head back to the Guild to let them know immediately and then work out the schedule of when we can get there and come back. The stones might take a while, but we can do it."

Asin lets out a low purr in agreement as the two leave the smiling Armorer behind. This will be interesting – Asin has never traveled to another city before, so the journey in itself will be a new experience. Traveling as guards will be boring if it is similar to their time in the Army, but she can accept that.

***

At the Adventurer's Guild, Daniel and Asin move over to the closest free attendant, quickly confirming their acceptance of the quest and the timetable for upcoming caravans traveling to Silverstone.

"Look, Asin; there's a caravan heading out in three days. They are even hiring, so we should be able to get hired and paid for the trip. Unfortunately, we might have to wait a little bit for the next trip back – looks like there's one that leaves a week before we're scheduled to arrive and not another one for at least another three weeks after that. We'll probably be gone then for…" Daniel frowns, trying to do the arithmetic in his head.

"Two months," chuffs Asin smirking.

"Right, two months. Well, not as bad as the three he mentioned, but it'll be a while. I wonder if we can get added as supplementary guards or something on the trip back…" Daniel frowns, scratching his chin. Three weeks of not being paid were viable for sure, but it would not be pleasant. Asin just shrugs, tapping the first schedule and pointing to the attendant. "Right, right. Let's get signed on first."

Once that is done, Daniel looks to Asin who points to the Dungeon. "Best we get working then. I've got a lot of debt to pay off!"

Asin lets out a low purr of humor, nodding aggressively and waving him on. Perhaps they could even locate the chest today – though they weren't entirely certain it made sense to try for it. Still, they could at least check out the danger.

Chapter 3

"Ready?" Daniel enquires, smiling slightly at Asin who nods back. Daniel turns back to Khy'ra who has stayed the night, pulling her close to give her one last kiss before she laughs, pushing him away. He would miss her.

"Daniel!" Elise calls out as the pair begin to walk out of the inn, and he turns, accepting the basket of food from the innkeeper gratefully. "You come back, okay? Both of you."

"It's just an escort quest, Elise!" Daniel says exasperatedly, shaking his head.

Khy'ra nods as well adding, "It's only two months. It'll be over in moments, just you wait."

As the two Adventurers head away, Elise mutters to her friend, "Not all of us live for hundreds of years, you know."

***

The caravan is pulled up in the merchant's quarter, a baker's dozen of wagons and a pair of well-appointed carriages arrayed before them. Waggoneers move back and forth, checking the load and their wagons, making last minute adjustments as they get ready for the long road ahead under the watchful eye of the permanent caravan guards. A smaller group of poorer travelers gather at the tail-end of the caravan on mules and horses and in a few cases, on foot. Those travelers have paid a small sum to come along with the caravan, sheltering in the additional protection offered by traveling in groups. However, the protection is minimal as the caravan guards are tasked with protecting the goods, not the people in the train. Still, it ensures that most wild animals will not bother them, and for those poor and desperate enough, the willing paid for the privilege of joining the caravan.

Walking together, Asin and Daniel weave forwards pass grumpy waggoneers and foot passengers in thread-bare clothing. As they arrive at the front of the caravan, they spot a small group of other Adventurers who await the pleasure of the caravan master.

The other four Adventurers are all humans dressed in a mixture of plate and leather armor except for the Priest in his blue cassock. Daniel makes a note of him, always happy to see another potential healer in a group. Asin in turn surveys the melee fighters, nose wrinkling as they near. Obviously, this group had spent insufficient time at the bath houses lately.

Finally, the caravan master stumps up to them. A florid-faced, blond-haired and overweight middle-aged man, he huffs and breathes deeply when he sees the group, "Karlak. I hate Karlak Adventurers. Not a single damn archer amongst you lot."

Daniel opens his mouth to protest then shuts it with a snap. The man had a point, and considering how truly awful a shot Daniel was with the crossbow, he felt it was better to stay silent.

"Right then. You lot get to ride with my waggoneers. Keep an eye out for monsters and bandits, fight them off as necessary. You get paid a daily wage for the time you spend with us, but only if you finish the journey. You get paid nothing if you leave before your appointed location.

"Food is included, but you should have your own bedroll and tent. Your task is to guard the wagons, my goods and my people in that order. The passengers in those carriages," the caravan master waves his hand to the two carriages, "are considered goods, so you guard them with your lives. You keep your hands to yourselves otherwise.

"Any questions? Then ask my lead waggoneer, Chip." A last gesture points to a grayed out, wizened man who sits on the front wagon, his face shaded by a wide-brimmed gray hat that looks as old and beaten as he is. "Don't speak with me again unless there's an attack."

His speech done, the caravan master stomps off, leaving the group somewhat surprised. After a moment, Daniel and Asin shrug and head over to Chip followed closely by the other group. Before they can even get to the old wagon leader, another waggoneer waves them over.

"Right, you two can ride with me. I'm third-in-line, and you can just add your bags to my wagon." A hand is stuck out with a wide smile, first offered to Asin and then Daniel. "I'm Gabriel, and I must say, I like the looks of you two."

"Uhh... Thanks. I'm Daniel, that's Asin," Daniel shakes the hand, glancing at the wagon and then to Chip who just offers a slight nod. Gabriel's vehicle was a covered wagon, and after a moment's more consideration, Daniel shrugs and tosses his bag inside and helps Asin get hers in. Asin then proceeds to crawl into the wagon itself, propping her foot up on a nearby chest and nodding to Daniel who gets on the front seat.

"So, what did you like?" Daniel enquires once Gabriel finishes fussing and gets on next to him.

"You're a small group. That's always good. Big groups, they get by because there's a lot of them. A small group like you, you're either very new or good," Gabriel explains and then nods to Daniel's arms. "And I ain't seen many newbie Adventurers with enchanted bracers."

"I guess you meet a lot of Adventurers in this job," Daniel says, mildly impressed at how quickly Gabriel has assessed the pair. As they inch through the streets of Karlak, Daniel lets his gaze wander over the familiar streets.

"Sure, lots. All the same though, you guys. No offense meant, but we do the circuit - the capital to the Gray Mountains to Silverstone and back to Warmount," Gabriel says, smiling. "After a while, you guys blend together. I can even tell you where that other group is going."

"Oh?" Daniel raises an eyebrow.

"Peel. It's about a week and a half and our first major stop. They've got a dungeon of their own, Beginner one like Karlak but smaller. It's actually got tougher monsters though, so most Adventurers from Karlak go there after they're done here. Good training grounds if you aren't entirely sure you want to try out a Journeyman's Dungeon yet."

Nodding in understanding, Daniel files the information away, watching as they slowly trundle along.

"Not that I mind your friend lounging back there, but once we're out of town the caravan master will want her out," Gabriel adds, and Daniel nods, turning to look back to Asin. She just gives him a nod, her sensitive hearing having picked up the words of caution.

"You know, that group reminds me of this other group we once picked up in Karlak. Well, they didn't have a Priest that group, just another fighter. The thing I remember about that fighter was his green leather armor - green! Why..." Gabriel begins, obviously relishing the chance to tell a story to a new audience.

Daniel nods along, curious to hear what Gabriel had to say. Certainly, the waggoneer had to have a different perspective than the Adventurers themselves.

***

It takes the caravan nearly half the day to get out of town, winding their way through crowded streets and then having each wagon inspected and sent on its way by the guards. During this time, Gabriel never stops expounding on story after story, only pausing long enough to swig water from his waterskin. Next to him, Daniel listens politely, pulling gently at his leather armor as the midday heat begins to get to him.

"Never understood why you Adventurers insist on wearing those things. Why I had this one Adventurer who would put on a full set of plate mail every morning…" Gabriel begins, and Daniel finally tunes him out, swigging at his waterskin as he stares at the rolling hills that surround the town of Karlak. Strange to think that only nine months ago he had come to town down these roads himself on another wagon to start his journey as an Adventurer.

He eyes the rolling hills, his stomach rumbling and looks up, noting how the sun has passed the zenith. "Are we not stopping for lunch?"

"Not a chance. Quidley hates wasting time, and we're behind schedule already getting out of town. We'll be traveling all through the day now to get to his favorite spot to camp at. As it stands, we'll probably arrive late in the day. Though, it does remind me of the time when we left Pilak…" Gabriel says, launching into another story.

"You know something, Gabriel? I think Asin should take the seat for a bit. I'm going to walk if you don't mind," Daniel interrupts the man, standing up. "Not used to these seats."

"No, it's good. I'll finish this one later." Gabriel smiles, watching Daniel hop down and dragging Asin forward reluctantly. On his feet, he walks alongside the wagon, letting his eyes roam over the countryside. This was going to be a long trip.

***

Talkative as Gabriel was, he was correct, and it was late in the evening when they finally reach their evening resting spot. Daniel eyes the campground and silently approves. It had very little to distinguish it from any other spot to those unused to travel, but it had a few good points. There was a small stream within a short distance that would provide the camp with easy access to water, the area around the campsite was relatively flat which meant setting up tents would be easy and watching for threats even easier. With only a small stand of trees blocking the view a short distance away, it would be hard to lay a trap here or sneak up on the caravan.

Even though this is the case, it does not stop Chip from directing the various wagons into a loose encirclement around the camp. As soon as the wagons are situated to the old waggoneer's satisfaction, the other waggoneers start unhitching horses and leading them gently to the stream. Daniel watches for a moment with Asin, unsure of what they should do. The pair are not the only lost souls, and they and the other guests are quickly chivvied into action by Chip who directs them on where to sleep and the cook fire that is to be theirs.

"Hi there, I'm Daniel, and this is Asin." Daniel offers his hand to the other four Adventurers when they all convene at the fire which Asin is working on getting started with practiced ease. "We were wondering how we'd be handling the camp chores? Both Asin and I are decent cooks, so we were thinking we could handle that?"

"I'm Marco, that's Delia, Dale, and Palmer," the tallest of the group who has added a dagger to his sword and shield style says, taking and shaking Daniel's hand. "And we'll take you up on that offer. Can you guys deal with lunch too?"

Asin nods firmly, the fire is started so she saunters away to talk to Chip about where to get their portion of the evening meal. Daniel chuckles, watching his friend move and notes the interested look Dale sends to Asin. "Asin doesn't talk much. Though I think that's my cue to get the water."

"Right, we'll get on the latrine then," Marco says and waves his friends away. Split off, the camp chores that they have to take care of are completed quickly with Chip coming by to assign watches for the group.

As Asin warms the water and pulls out a pan to cook the slices of meat they have drawn from stores and warm up their bread, Daniel spots Palmer standing to the side surrounded by various waggoneers and working his healing magic on their assorted ailments. As Daniel watches, coin passes hands, and he turns away, his lips twisting wryly. For a moment Daniel considers helping out, but he dismisses the thought as being too petty. Just because the Priest was willing to take money did not mean that his actions were not justified. Instead he stood up to wander the perimeter.

To the south where they came from, he finds the grouping of poorer travelers getting ready to rest. He watches them for a short time, noticing how some struggle with the simplest of camp duties like setting up tents or starting a fire and he mentally sighs at the city folk. As one particularly burly and well-dressed man attempts to add a densely leafed, newly cut branch to a fire, he hurries over to help.

It is only when Delia comes over, mentioning that dinner is ready, that Daniel realizes how long he has been helping out. A few last words of advice quickly become another fifteen minutes, and by the time he gets back, his food is cold. As Daniel sits with his cold food, he makes a mental note though to make a quick trip back when he is done - there were a few injuries and illnesses among that group that could benefit from a quick healing spell. After all, Daniel justifies to himself, he had no use for his mana tonight. It had nothing to do with a particularly pretty young lady smiling at him.

Chapter 4

For a week and a half, the duo travel with the caravan, visiting a couple of villages along the way. They rarely stop longer than an hour or two at these villages, long enough for various waggoneers to buy and sell their goods before moving on, draining the villagers dry of coin. These villages are the lucky ones - located on main thoroughfares they receive relatively regular visits from caravans of wagons which can provide much needed raw materials and goods. Other villages further out or on less well-traveled paths have to make do with the occasional trader. For those villagers who cannot wait, a trip to the lucky thoroughfare villages will be required to meet the caravans on their scheduled runs. It is why Quidley has pushed the caravan each day, doing his best to keep to his posted timetable. After all, a prompt caravan sees the most customers.

Peel is a small town, smaller even than Karlak, though it has stone walls - or parts of one at least. The wall was built such that the bottom half was made of stone, wooden posts sandwiched between the stone exterior. As funds and materials became available, the next level of stone was added to the walls, strengthening the entire construction. Instead of entering the small town with the entire caravan, Quidley directs many to park outside while only a few wagons that have business in the town enter it. In this way, the waggoneers avoids the entry fee, parking the wagons in a nearby clearing outside the walls. As they pull in for the night, Chip waves the Adventurers over, four small pouches held in hand.

"Right, you four, this is your pay. Quidley will let the Guild know you've completed your Quest as agreed upon," Chip says as he hands the pouches over to the other Adventuring group before turning to speak with Asin and Daniel. "You two are free to visit the town if you wish, we'll be here for the rest of the day and tomorrow. If you intend to leave, you'll need to be back first thing in the morning two days from now."

"Okay," Daniel says and then looks over to Asin who jerks her head to town immediately. Yes, definitely time to check out a new town. Chip just snorts, their answer being entirely within his expectations. Together the pair trudge down to town after saying some hasty goodbyes. At the gate, they pay their entrance fee and head immediately for the town center without discussion. The town center would be where the Adventurer's Guild, the Dungeon, and inns that catered to Adventurers were located. Inns nearer the city entrance were mostly for the merchants, those who had no real desire to explore the town itself. Not that either of them intended to explore the city per se, their hearts and minds set on the new Dungeon.

"Adventurer's Guild first?" Daniel enquires and Asin nods. Inside, the Guild gives a great sense of deja vu, so similar is it to the layout of the one in Karlak that Daniel almost expects there to be a red-haired, bookish attendant working behind the counter. Instead, a matronly older woman sits flipping through a book looking bored.

"Afternoon," Daniel says as he walks up with Asin in tow. "We just arrived and were hoping you could tell us a little about the Dungeon."

"You're from Karlak, right? Five levels, only one kind of monster. All our levels are full levels, no chests on each floor but each floor has its own champion. In Peel, the monsters you'll face are lizardmen - you'll meet workers, scouts, hunters, warriors, champions, chieftains and warlocks. That's in order of difficulty. What levels are you?" the woman intones, never even looking up from her book.

"Uhh… six," Daniel answers quickly, and Asin adds, "Eight" to which Daniel starts, looking at his companion. He knew he had lost a level, but had she always been a level higher than him?

"Right then, you shouldn't go past level three, and the third level is pushing it. We've got wider corridors so expect ranged weaponry," the woman says. "Also, we close at eight."

Daniel and Asin share a bemused smile before asking together, "Traps?"

"Pitfall, deadfalls, darts and poison gas in the lowest levels. The first level has pitfalls, each level after that adds one more type in order," the attendant says.

"Ummm… How about mana crystals? Size and type?" Daniel asks.

"Grade D Level 8 to start," she declares and sighs, finally looking up. "That's all that I can tell you. The rest you will have to learn yourself."

Daniel and Asin share another look, a bit put-off by the rude and brusque attendant. However, she is correct - there isn't much more that either can think of to ask. Wishing her well, the two Adventurers leave for the Dungeon entrance, nodding to the guards and registering themselves before walking into the Dungeon. Both of them feel a slight chill of anticipation and find themselves grinning in excitement. This is, after all, their second ever dungeon.

***

"Down," Asin chuffs and Daniel crouches, a pair of throwing knives flashing past his head to bury in the lizardman's chest. Daniel straightens his knees immediately, catching the spear thrust on his shield and stepping forward to deal with the monster. Unfortunately, the lizardman steps back again, thrusting with its rusty spear and forcing Daniel to protect himself. He exhales hastily, drawing a deep breath to fill his lungs as he steps forward again in an attempt to force the monster back, frustration leaking through his control.

This was the third lizardman that they had met. In both other cases, the much wider and taller gray stone corridors of the Peel dungeon had allowed the two Adventurers to flank the creatures, rendering the monsters spears less effective. Unfortunately, they had the bad luck to encounter this particular creature in a smaller, narrower service corridor and were forced to fight him single file. Unable to flank the monster, the pair has to work at whittling it down gradually.

Daniel has pushed the creature three-quarters of the way back, receiving only a light gash on his arm for his trouble but the creature's longer spear has ensured that he cannot close in and finish the monster. Every time he attempts to do so the monster step backs. Stuck behind him, Asin is unable to attack effectively and is forced to take occasional pot-shots.

However, that was about to change as the Lizardman Worker realized it had now been backed up nearly towards the exit. It hisses, the stabbing of the spear getting more agitated as it attempts to keep Daniel back. This is a mistake as Daniel takes a particularly wide strike on the edge of his shield, pushing against the shaft of the spear to pin it against the wall. This allows him time to step in and lash out with his mace, sweat flying from his brow as he twists. The mace swings upwards, biting into the lizardman's body and sending it sprawling backward. Asin hops forward and passes Daniel in the small gap that is created, jumping directly onto the monster's body and jabbing her knives into its prone form, twisting them to add to the damage. Asin snarls slightly, the slightly too smooth skin of the creature disturbing under her furred knees. As it dies, a brief flare of light surrounds the body, and it dissolves, leaving its mana crystal behind.

Daniel breathes deeply, eyeing the crude wooden spear with distaste and letting it fall to the ground. Once again, he wishes he has access to the

Adventurers Level 10 Class Skill - Inventory. Without it, neither of them can safely store the spear for resale, and so they have to leave it aside, content with their earnings of mana stones.

Once Daniel catches his breath, the pair continue deeper into the dungeon to find the Level Champion. If the fight goes well, they hope to attempt the second level today as well, though it truly depends on how quickly they can finish this level. Both Adventurers move along the broad stone corridors quickly, Asin's quick eyes having spotted and alerted Daniel of the way the pitfall traps were made of slightly discolored stones early on. Now, even Daniel can pick them out with relative regularity, allowing the pair to move faster.

***

The differences in the Peel Dungeon did not end at the stone corridors and lizardmen monsters, as even the first floor was much larger and more expansive than their own. Traversing through the corridors, the pair have to fight numerous times before they finally manage to stumble across the Champion's location, after hours of exploration. Together, both Adventurers pull their heads back from the doorway leading into the room after quickly scoping out the Lizardman Champion and another worker. The two Adventurers look at each other before Daniel is the first to speak, "Champion's mine, Miss Level 8."

He smirks at her and Asin rolls her eyes but nods, hefting a throwing knife in her left hand and one of her longer knives in her right. She waits for Daniel to ready himself and then, together, they dash around the corner. Asin activates her Piercing Shot, throwing it at the Lizardman Worker before sprinting over as she draws her other long knife, engaging the creature in close combat. Her first throw drills into the Worker's shoulder, making it hiss in anger.

Daniel charges at the Champion alone, taking the few moments he needs to cross the distance to further observe the monster. The Lizardman Champion wields a better-crafted spear and stands nearly six feet tall, looming over the shorter Adventurer. Covered in dark green scales and wearing a torn, red tunic over its torso and legs, the Champion jabs the spear towards Daniel to keep him away. Hours of fighting spear wielders has taught Daniel some new tricks however, and, instead of catching the spear with his shield, he bats the spear head aside to the left with his mace and continues to close the distance. The spear now out of alignment, he shoves his shield outwards at an angle, riding the spear shaft down even as the Champion retracts his blow. Once he has firm contact, Daniel grins and engages Shield Bash, slamming the spear even further off-course and making the Champion fight to keep hold of its weapon. Unfortunately, the spear does not conduct the lightning that dances on his shield to the monster, but he still succeeds in his main objective - to close the rest of the distance unharmed.

Daniel is now in range, and he immediately triggers his Double Strike skill, sending his mace smashing once then again onto the Champion's head and shoulders. The blows are only partially blocked by a raised claw that has released its grip on the spear. The claw is crushed, and the monster drops its now useless spear to the side, the greater length of the weapon difficult to wield single-handed and in close combat. Instead, the Champion attempts to use its claws to swipe at Daniel. Daniel ducks to the side, then kicks the creature in the legs, upsetting its balance further before laying into it again with his mace. Keeping the pressure up, he smashes his mace into the Champion again and again before the creature falls over, dead.

Slightly out of breath, Daniel grins and looks over to Asin who has finished her monster. The staircase down is just in front of them but it is late, and after a brief discussion, they agree to test the next floor out tomorrow. They will head downstairs, activate the Dungeon glyph and then return to the inn. Better to hand in their money now and get a good night's sleep.

***

Up early in the morning, Daniel and Asin meet up for a quick breakfast that they barely taste as they cram the food into their mouths. Without a word, they grab the pre-packed lunches they requested from the Inn and head out with a bounce in their steps. Day two of a new dungeon and a new level to boot. What could be better?

The second floor is very similar to the first, its wide gray stone corridors lit by the soft glow of mana imbued stone all around them. A slight breeze could be felt if they paid attention, bringing a dry, slightly sour smell through the level. Corridors turn into rooms where Lizardmen wait, in groups of two or three, playing a game of sticks, training, eating and on one occasion napping.

After the sixth such room, Daniel turns to Asin, murmuring, "This is so strange. It feels less like a Dungeon and more like, well, more like it's their home."

Asin nods at that, scratching at her cheek. It really did feel like they'd invaded the Lizardmen's home and were uncouth, ill-mannered and violent guests, killing their way through their unsuspecting hosts. It felt wrong, even though they both knew that this was a Dungeon. The Lizardmen weren't real; they left no bodies when killed and yet they could not shake the feeling.

For a time, the two stare at each other, battling the strangeness of it all. In the end, they shrug and focus, knowing that as strange as this is, the Lizardmen needed to be killed. Left alone too long, they would spill out of the Dungeon into the town, the corruption induced by Ba'al given a chance to spread. Eventually, such a Dungeon might be the start of a new Blight if left unchecked for too long. It was their job, however strange it seemed, to kill these Lizardmen before it happened.

They move on, pushing through the Dungeon and its monsters, their faces set and the bounce in their steps gone. Experienced Adventurers had a saying - that each new level taught a different lesson, each Dungeon a different experience. In Peel, it seemed the lesson was that whatever they felt, whatever they believed, they still had a job to do.

Focused now, the two work their way through the Dungeon, Asin testing for traps, and Daniel watching for Lizardmen Scouts. The Scouts were annoying as half of them were armed with crossbows, able to attack at range. It forced both Adventurers to move slowly, especially after the first deadfall that Daniel had landed in trying to chase a Scout down. It was only luck and the application of healing magic that allowed him to continue delving today, though the experience forced them to slow down significantly.

The only truly difficult fight comes three-quarters of the day in as they rest in a room for a quick break. As they rest, the Lizardman Scout Champion leans into the room from the doorway, lines up a shot, and fires at Asin. Only their wariness and Asin's quick reflexes allow her to roll out of the way with a long scratch as her only injury. Daniel struggles to his feet quickly, putting his shield in front of him and the two follow the Champion's quickly retreating figure carefully. Annoyed and angry, the two still remember the lessons of the day, making sure to check every passageway for traps and ambushes even as they slowly chase down the Champion. It takes them hours, working their way to the Champion as Daniel blocks the bolts it fires and Asin throws her knives, whittling down the Champion whenever it stops to attack them.

In the end, the Champion can only limp away, out of tricks entirely. It has dragged them into other rooms where Lizardmen wait, through trap-filled corridors and on a long chase through a series of twisting passages in an attempt to escape but now it is finally brought to heel. Out of bolts, out of tricks, it falls to Daniel's mace in short order.

By this time, it is late, and the two Adventurers are exhausted. They journey up to town to sell their mana stones; another lesson learned this long day in blood and frustration. Before they leave, Daniel puts his money down for a new light crossbow with bolts. It is time to learn how to shoot. As for Asin, she comes back with a trio of bolos, chuffing to herself as she spins them around.

***

Dinner is a quiet affair; the two Adventurers exhausted from their days working the new dungeon. They had pushed hard to do as much as they could, but their lack of equipment and preparedness had stymied their ability to truly progress. Still, they were relatively uninjured, alive and though slightly poorer at least had new weapons.

Daniel smiles at his friend, raising a glass of wine to her and she purrs, sipping on hers. If nothing else, this inn had a good wine selection. They sit alone, the other patrons avoiding their table in the corner and eyeing Asin with trepidation. It seems Peel has an even smaller population of Beastkin than Karlak and while the patrons were mostly Adventurers, none desire to mix with the Beastkin.

As they are finishing up their dinner, a pair of familiar faces wander into the tavern looking the worst for wear. Black-haired Delia, her sword in its sheath but lacking her shield and Palmer, limping and holding his side around his green robes stumble in and find a seat at a free table. Adventurers turn, eye the pair and then dismiss them from their mind, their injuries and hangdog expressions telling the tale.

Asin turns to look at Daniel who sighs and nods, both of them approaching the table cradling the last of their mugs. Daniel takes the lead, murmuring, "Evening."

It takes a few silent moments before Delia looks up, staring at Daniel with blank eyes before a spark of interest kindles, "Daniel. And the Cat.

You look well. I guess you didn't do the dungeons…"

"Umm…" Daniel pauses, watching as Palmer winces and tugs at the bandage ineffectually. "Here, let me do that." Quick work is made of fixing the bandage, Palmer gritting his teeth as the bandage is pulled tight around his body and then secured. Briefly, Daniel considers using his Gift, having exhausted all his Mana the moment they had left the Dungeon to heal his and Asin's minor wounds. Briefly, but none of their wounds were life-threatening, just painful.

"How far did you get?" Daniel asks.

"We managed to make it to the fourth today. First few floors weren't hard, so we rushed through them. The third floor was tough, but the Lizardmen, they would stand and fight. But the fourth-floor Champion, he had these Scouts with him. They kept shooting us and shooting us, we couldn't get away, couldn't run…" Delia says, shaking her head. "I told him to wait, told him we should take our time. Marco said we could do it though, said we'd be fine. He cried when they cut off his arm…"

"I'm sorry." Daniel sits down next to her, offering the comfort of his presence. Asin leaves, coming back a few minutes later with beers for the group which are greedily taken and emptied by the two beaten Adventurers. A short while later a waitress comes by, depositing the evening's special.

"I told him," Delia says, poking at the food. Palmer avoids all their gazes, working industriously at his meal, his hands occasionally beginning to tremble before he brings them under control. After a time, Daniel and Asin stand, murmuring a goodbye. As they leave, Daniel wonders if the pair will team up with others now, perhaps someone with ranged weaponry. Death as an Adventurer was a part of life, no matter how experienced you were. Losing a friend, though, was never easy, no matter how inured you were to the realities of the world they had chosen.

Chapter 5

The next morning sees both Asin and Daniel standing beside the caravan at the crack of dawn. Neither having been given an exact time the wagons would leave, they decided to arrive early instead. The moment he spots them, Gabriel waves to the pair and beckons them over to his wagon.

In a corner of the campground, the caravan master is offering his usual, cordial welcome to a new group of Adventurers from Peel. Asin watches the group intently. They are made up of a large yellow-furred Catkin and a pair of human Adventurers. The first human Adventurer wields a sword and shield but the second seems to favor a short sword and bow combination and wears a mottled brown-green cloak. All three adventurers are dressed in a mix of plate and chainmail armor that is worn but still serviceable. Even to the novice Adventurers, they can tell that the weapons and armor are a couple of quality levels higher than theirs. Asin nudges Daniel, nodding to the group to get his attention before purring, "Ranger."

Daniel looks over and spots the Ranger and nods slightly in turn. The Ranger was a rare sight as the famously taciturn and independent Adventurers kept to the borders of Brad. On the other hand, they were known as well for their ability with the bow, and Daniel rubs at his jaw, thinking of how to approach him for help.

"Well, it's good that you returned. Wasn't sure if you would - we lose about half our guards who are supposed to return to us in Peel," Gabriel grouses as he hops on the wagon after hitching the horses to it. "Why, this one time, we had this fair-haired buxom young lass of an Adventurer, all clad in plate who was supposed to be with us to Silverstone. She arrived in Peel and what do you know, she meets up with this sorcerer and priest and they go Adventuring in the Dungeon! Never joins up with us again. Real pity on that too, she sure was pretty. Still, I figure if I had a chance to work with a sorcerer and a priest, I'd join them myself. Especially since I hear they were all women."

The moment Gabriel begins to speak, Asin flashes a grin at Daniel and scrambles to her customary perch at the top of the wagon, her tail lazily waving alongside the canvas top as she sits on the wagon and works on her claws. Daniel glares at the traitor before turning back to Gabriel and his never-ending stories, trying to set his face to an attentive position.

***

That evening as they come to a stop, Daniel makes his way past the outlying wagons to the nearby river to wash. Stripped to his undergarments, Daniel completes the ritual quickly, shivering in the cold emerald glacial runoff of the river and laying the thick mat of soap leaves aside. He scrambles out of the water, shaking his blocky frame to free it of excess water before squatting to begin washing his clothing.

At the snap of a twig, Daniel spins, grabbing for his nearby mace. The young lady who surprised him yelps, dropping her washing basket and laundry before blushing furiously at his half-naked state. Realizing it is just one of the hanger-on's, Daniel smiles at her and lowers the mace to his side. "It's okay."

The young brunette with the cute, pert nose shakes her head, hastily picking up the washing. "No, no. I'm sorry."

"Yvette, isn't it?" Daniel says, smiling to the woman as he reaches for and pulls on the extra pair of pants he brought along. She nods jerkily, still not meeting his gaze. "I'm just washing my clothes; you're welcome to join me."

She blushes again and nods, coming over and squatting a short distance from him. She takes out the clothing she brought, focusing on it. Daniel returns to what he was doing, catching the sideway glances the young lady shoots him occasionally. A part of him preens at the attention, a small smile lighting on his face unknowingly. Noticing the rather large amount of clothing she is washing, Daniel says, "Are you washing that for others, Yvette?"

Yvette nods jerkily, blushing again before she looks at Daniel's manhandling of his clothes. She speaks up, hesitantly and shyly, "I could wash yours too. For free."

"Oh, I couldn't ask you to do that," Daniel replies immediately, shaking his clothes and grimacing at the hole he spots.

"No, it's fine. I could mend that too," she raises her voice, nodding. "I have skills in Housekeeping and Sewing, and you've been so kind, healing us. Please?"

Daniel blinks, considering her offer. He really was very bad at sewing - his last attempt had already torn and while he earned more as an Adventurer, paying for new clothing was a constant headache due to the amount of damage they received. In addition, his work in the Clinic had made him realize that allowing others to help or pay him actually made them feel better as well. It was one reason why Khy'ra had a flexible payment policy in the Clinic. "If you're sure. Thank you."

Yvette smiles, stands up quickly and walks over to take his clothing from him. As she does so, her hand brushes against his and she blushes, backing away quickly and ducking her head, embarrassed about her calloused and rough fingers. "I'll… I'll get it right back to you tomorrow when it's done. If that's okay?"

Daniel nods to her, standing around for a moment unsure. "So, uhhh…. Where are you traveling to?"

"Silverstone," she replies promptly. "My father, he's a Master mason. He was offered a job at the new temple they're building."

"A Master mason? That's impressive." Daniel echoes her voice, his gaze resting on the small, pert frame before him, eyes tracking over the way the clothing presses against her body. "And you?"

"I'm… well, I'm just with him for now. My mother, she died a while ago, and I help my Da keep the house while he works." Again Yvette blushes. "He says, well, I'll be a good housewife one day. And you? You're an Adventurer?" Realizing how stupid that sounds, Yvette hides her face in her washing again, not daring to look at Daniel.

"Yes. Just under a year actually," Daniel replies, slowly stretching an arm as he talks to her. Yvette looks over her shoulder at a grunt and notices Daniel with his arm over his head, stretching, and her eyes track over his muscular, hairless chest. Eyes lock on a pocked puncture wound just under a floating rib, and Daniel answers the unasked question. "Crawler in Karlak. They have these big pincers and this one bit right through my armor. Hurt like hell and healing, well, it left that."

Of course, he could have healed it fully and removed the scar, but Daniel had decided long ago to avoid such healings. It created a significant strain on his Gift to do so and wasn't worth the effort. So long as he could move and fight without pain, anything more was unnecessary. It also headed off any requests for cosmetic healings which he really did not want to deal with.

"Oh, you're so brave," Yvette says, looking down at her hands. "I could never do that."

"Well, it's not for everyone," Daniel answers, shaking his head. "But I don't think it's brave, not really. It's not as if farmers or miners aren't in danger outside of Dungeons, and at least we carry weapons."

Yvette nods dumbly along to Daniel's words, putting aside the latest shirt and moving to the next one. Unsure of what else to say, Daniel ends up saying, "I should get back. I've got to get dinner going."

"I'll see you," Yvette whispers and when Daniel has left, quickly hugs the shirt, amazed at how bold she was.

***

When Daniel arrives back at the camp, he is surprised to find Asin cooking and speaking with the Catkin, the two sharing quiet purrs and growls. He blinks for a moment before shaking his head, moving to put away his cleaning supplies. At his bag, he stares down at his newly acquired weapon, picking up the crossbow and bolts before surveying the area for a good spot.

Setting up a small distance from others, where a small hillock and a fallen tree provide him with a target, Daniel grunts, and strains as he works the crossbow back. Adjusting his stance, Daniel draws a deep breath and exhales, focusing on the half-remembered lessons he received when they joined the Army. As he exhales, Daniel releases the bolt and watches it wing away to dig into the ground four feet short of the target. Pushing aside the rising irritation, Daniel works to cock the crossbow again. Practice. He just needed practice.

Thirty minutes later after having shot through all his bolts twice, Daniel is sweating and swearing. The target was only fourty yards away, and he still had not managed to hit it even once.

"You. This. It's embarrassing." The Ranger walks up, shaking his head at Daniel and unable to watch the young man practice any further. The Ranger is dressed clad in his mottled green and brown cloak, though with the hood thrown back Daniel can see the young, unlined face beneath it and friendly brown eyes. "Let me help you, or else the guards will never let us Adventurers live this down."

At the mention of the guards, Daniel looks back to the camp, having forgotten about everyone else as he practiced. He realizes that more than a few guards have been watching him, a few openly laughing at his lack of progress. Embarrassed, Daniel turns away quickly and looks at the Ranger imploringly. "Please!"

"Right then, let's start with your stance," the Ranger states, moving up to Daniel and correcting his stance. Daniel nods, focusing on what the Ranger says. He certainly needed to improve.

***

"Well, that's… better?" Iyas, the Ranger says with a resigned tone. The evening had progressed such that even in the long summer days, their practice had to be called to an end. "Gather the bolts, and I'll show you how to care for them and the crossbow."

Daniel nods, staring at his target. Well, he had winged the tree at last. The added pressure had made his first few tries after Iyas arrived even worse than before, but now, now he was beginning to get it. Hurrying forward, Daniel moves to collect his bolts, lips twisting in disgust as he notes one shattered shaft. As he hurries back from his task, he sees Asin still deep in her conversation with her Catkin friend, a hand on the other Adventurer's lap. As he hurries over to the camp, his stomach rumbles and he realizes that he has not eaten. Looking over to Iyas, he points to the cooking pot and the other Adventurer nods.

Having slurped his slightly burnt dinner down, Daniel returns to the Ranger who shows him how to care for the bolts, replacing fletching and ensuring that the bolts were still straight. He even pulls out a stick to show Daniel how he can even make his own if he cares to, though he points out that Daniel will need a carving knife for that. Daniel watches with intensity, soon taking a direct hand and checking over his bolts as Iyas carves.

"You and your Catkin friend, you're both a bit junior to be leaving Karlak aren't you?" Iyas says as he continues to focus on his carving.

"I guess? We're on a fetch quest actually, to Silverstone and back," Daniel explains, tongue stuck between his teeth as he works on a new feather.

"Ah! I remember those. I used to run a number of them before I joined Niko and Tevfik," Iyas says smiling. "I can't say I miss them at all.

Paid good, especially on the Borderlands, but quite boring."

Daniel shrugs, holding up the bolt to inspect. Iyas looks up, shakes his head and Daniel sighs and tries again. "It's our first. We did a few Hunt and Gather quests while in Karlak, but this is our first."

"Well, Rangers are more suited for them," Iyas offers, and then adds, "It's good to get out though, see the world a bit. Too many new Adventurers just fall into the routine of only working Dungeons."

Daniel smiles, basking slightly at the more experienced Adventurers praise. "Why were you in Peel? You three don't seem, you know, of the right level."

Iyas laughs. "Yes. We're not Beginners anymore, but are you aware that you get a minor experience boost for each Dungeon you clear?" Daniel shakes his head, and Iyas continues, "You do. It's why even experienced Adventurers will clear beginner dungeons. Of course, it also helps to keep Ba'al's influence down."

Daniel nods, thinking over what Iyas said and then holds up the next bolt. Getting confirmation from Iyas, he smiles and turns to the next one.

***

"Morning, Asin, you're up with me today, are you?" Gabriel chatters away to Asin as he climbs on the wagon, clicking his tongue right after to start the horses moving. "Always nice to have you up, though you aren't much of a conversationalist. That's okay though, my Ma always said I could talk enough for two, and with you, I'll need to!

"Well now, we're on the way to the village of Stolin. I bet you haven't heard about Stolin, have you? Small little village, we wouldn't even stop there normally, but it is the only village this side of the border for a good four days. Right in the middle of the plains with all the wheat fields, so that's what we'll be driving through for a bit. Not much to see but the sky and the wheat really, not for a few days. Why you'll get so bored about seeing wheat, you'll want to cry. Reminds of that time when Pini started nodding off on his wagon and drove it right into the ditch. Well, you know Pini, he carries…"

Thoroughly pleased with himself, Daniel slows down to let the wagon pass him by as he walks along the road. He grinned slightly, just happy to be on his feet and away from the chatterbox. He would walk exclusively, but being paid to guard the caravan meant that Daniel needed to be rested enough to deal with problems if they arose. Not that anything major had happened as yet. The worst had been a horse that had tripped and broken its foot when it saw a snake.

True to Gabriel's word, they walk through plains of light green grass and fields of newly sprouted wheat for the next few hours. The land around them slowly shifts from the rolling plains interspersed with stands of trees to flat land divided into occasional managed farm lots.

Unimpeded, a strong wind constantly blows, tugging at canvas straps and clothing alike and ruffling the stalks of grass and wheat. The wind carries a hint of morning chill along with the scent of freshly turned earth, newly grown grass and last evening's quick rain shower. Above, the sky almost goes on forever, seeming to stretch on and on before being finally bracketed by the distant mountains in the North.

Walking beneath the sky, Daniel hunches slightly, unused to such a sky. Born in the foothills of the mountains to the North, he was always more comfortable in the forest or underground. Still, at least the plains have the advantage of making travel safe - it would be impossible for bandits and monsters to hide. Tired of walking, Daniel hurries up to jump onto the wagon bed, swinging his feet up and letting the creak of the wagon wheels and the drone of Gabriel's incessant talk wash over him.

A scream breaks Daniel from his reverie, the sound originating from behind the caravan. He hops down from his seat, grabbing his mace and moving to the side of the road as he scans for danger. Two wagons behind, Iyas has climbed onto a wagon top and is scanning the horizon before he releases the tension in his bow, shaking his head Waggoneers relax as the experienced Adventurer gives an all clear as do the guards. Watching everyone relax, Daniel decides to hurry to the back where the foot passengers walk, and the scream originated.

Pushing past the crowd, Daniel finds a young man crying and holding his broken leg. Another helpful citizen has attempted to straighten it, badly, and Daniel hisses in frustration. Pushing the man aside, he grunts a quick warning before reaching forward and realigning the bones. He follows this by channeling a Minor Healing. The swelling begins to reduce, torn flesh and bone knitting before their eyes.

"What happened?" Daniel asks, testing along the edges of the initial break. Luckily the bone had not fragmented so healing it was a simple matter that required only a single casting of his spell. "Can someone find some straight sticks? We'll need to provide the leg some support."

"Basher rabbit," the reply comes from behind Daniel, the voice surprisingly high-pitched. Daniel looks over and blinks, seeing the third Adventurer of the group, the swordsman standing there. The swordsman is tall, maybe as much as a foot taller than Daniel with a slight scar near the corner of one hazel eye. "Probably got startled and attacked."

Daniel nods, casting one last minor healing before quickly strapping the leg to the supporting sticks. "The leg will be tender for the next few weeks. You shouldn't put too much weight on it, but…" Daniel nods to the caravan that is already a distance away. "Well, just come and see me tonight and I'll see what I can do."

The peasant grabs Daniel's hand in his, murmuring thanks before standing with the help of his friends. Daniel sighs, flashing a smile at

Yvette who he spots standing with her father before turning to the Adventurer who is still watching him.

"So, you're a Healer, eh?" the swordsman says, his hand resting casually on the pommel of his hand-and-a-half sword.

"In a way." Daniel glances at the group who are moving and begins to walk as well, hurrying to get back to the wagons with the swordsman alongside him.

"Interesting. I'm Niko," the swordsman introduces himself as he joins Daniel.

"Daniel."

"Most Adventurers don't take the time to learn enough healing to pick up the Minor Healing spell," Niko adds, looking at Daniel from the corner of his eyes as he walks. "You're pretty unusual actually."

"I don't really understand why though," admits Daniel after a moment. "It's so useful."

"Ah, it's a matter of time and opportunity. Few Healers are willing to spend time teaching those who aren't going to be Healers since it's so time-intensive and for those who can find a teacher, it still takes a long time to reach the required skill level. The way I understand it, to even get started you need about five levels in healing," Niko explains. "Most Adventurers just find it easier to train in their primary skillsets and become better at that, though of course, we all pick up a level or two in healing, eventually."

Daniel nods rubbing his chin. His Gift had allowed him to bypass much of the initial learning stages, teaching him aspects of the body and how it worked on an almost intuitive level. He recalled how surprised the visiting Healer at the mine was at the young boy's knowledge. During his short visits, the Healer had always done his best to teach and convince Daniel to become a Healer himself, becoming ultimately unsuccessful. Now, for a moment, Daniel feels guilty for the time the old man spent with him, guilty about his life choice. He could have been, should have been a Healer. Yet…

"You two!" Chip shouts at them, breaking Daniel from his thoughts. "Who told you to leave the caravan? You aren't being paid to guard them!"

Daniel winces, pulling himself to attention as Chip continues to harangue them for slacking off on their duties. Niko just nods his head, occasionally offering a verbal acknowledgment. When the grumpy, wrinkled old man is not looking he rolls his eyes at Daniel to express his own frustration. Daniel has to cough to cover a chuckle, working hard to keep a straight face as Chip continues to scold them.

Released at last, the two Adventurers bid goodbye to each other and take up their spaces in the wagon train, though Daniel finds himself seated in the front. Asin gives him a wink as he passes her by, chewing on the slice of dried sausage.

***

As promised, Stolin is a small village with a single-room tavern, a blacksmith and a sundry goods shop dominating the town center. Next to the tavern stands a large bare field where the wagons are directed to park, the caravan master and a select few being allowed to sleep in the tavern. The rest are assigned to the ground around the caravan itself while a few wagons turn off, heading in the direction of the lone mill and the grain barns.

Asin waves Daniel aside as she grabs the cookpot and their empty water skins; Tevfik prowls up to join her at the river with his team's supplies. Daniel smiles slightly, noting how close the two are to each other already, heading towards the woodpile.

"Hi…" the hesitant, sweet voice behind him makes Daniel turn away from the fire he is slowly coaching to light. He smiles as he spots Yvette who holds his washed and darned clothing in her arms. She blushes slightly at the smile, thrusting the pile towards him. The moment he takes it, she blushes again and scurries off, leaving Daniel to watch her swaying behind. He quickly turns away though when he catches her father's glare and has to remind himself that there is nothing wrong with looking.

Smiling slightly, Daniel returns to watching the fire as he waits for Asin to return. And waits. And waits. Growling in impatience after a long hour, he stands and looks around, wondering where his friend is. It should not take this long to get water! Just as he is about to head to the river himself, he spots her hurrying back, fur and clothing disheveled with the full cookpot.

"Where are the water skins?" Daniel asks as he places the pot on the fire. Asin lets out a yowl of surprise and then ducks her head, spinning back and hurrying to the river. As Daniel watches her hurry off, he notes Tevfik is sauntering back like a cat that has eaten all the cream. Just like a cat…

Daniel chuckles to himself, wondering how Khy'ra would react to this news. At the thought of the beautiful blonde elf, he recalls another, much closer young female and ducks his head in embarrassment. Right, he had a girlfriend of sorts.

***

"We don't serve their kind," the older matron snaps at Daniel. Situated behind the kegs of beer that her husband had rolled out for the thirsty waggoneers, she points to Asin and Tevfik. "No better than animals they are. Why, young Ingrid says she saw the two of them rolling around near the river, yowling and doing what animals do. Disgusting!"

Daniel glares at her, tapping the table with his coin, "Well, is my money bad then?"

"No," the tavern keeper's wife says as she shakes her head to move some of her graying blonde hair from her eyes.

"Then I'll take three," says Daniel.

Eyes narrowing, she waves him away. "I changed my mind. You're not welcome either."

"You just said my money is good," Daniel says, tapping the coin on the table again.

"Well, it's not now, Beast lover." She sniffs and looks past him to the person behind. "You want a drink?"

Daniel shifts, placing himself in front of her gaze again. "Three mugs."

"Go away, or else I'll call my husband," the woman snaps at him.

"Go on then," Daniel challenges and then feels a hand drop on his shoulder. He turns and finds Tevfik shaking his head, pulling him along. Daniel resists for a moment but finds the other Adventurer stronger than him and is forced to move. The tavern keeper's wife snickers even as she pours the next drink.

"Why did you do that?"

"Not worth it, young one. They will not serve you or us and insisting they do will only cause trouble. We wouldn't want to be left behind by the caravan master," Tevfik says, finally letting go of Daniel now that they are away from the tavern. "Come, we've got drink."

"The wagon master wouldn't..." Daniel begins then closes his mouth as Asin just shoots him a disbelieving look. His lips twist, and he growls, knowing that they are right. They were just Adventurers - the village, on the other hand, was the caravan master's livelihood. It would not really be a choice.

"I am glad you care for us, but we are used to such things," Tevfik says as they join the fire where the other Adventurers sit. He disappears into the wagon, pulling a wineskin from his bag and handing it over.

"It's still not right," Daniel grumbles and the others laugh at the naiveté of the young man. Daniel just glares at them back before drinking from the wineskin, coughing at the harsh burn of the unexpectedly sweet but potent drink inside. This was no wine. It was Sabu, the Beastkin's alcoholic beverage of choice.

"Right or not, it is what it is. It will be many years before they accept us." Tevfik shrugs and takes back the wineskin from Daniel, handing it over to Asin whose nose is twitching already at the pungent smell. "Now, come! Tell us about yourself. Asin says you were part of the army's recent Orc Raid subjugation. We were too late to join that."

Somewhat mollified by the better alcohol, Daniel hesitantly tells the tale to his audience who in turn offer some tales of their own adventures. Eventually, a small crowd joins them, listening to the tales of derring-do that are passed back and forth between the Adventurers, the wineskin slowly being emptied.

Chapter 6

Wincing in the harsh morning light, Daniel lets out a little groan and attempts to roll out from underneath the wagon he crawled under for sleep. He blinks, staring at the young lady who is trapping his arm, Daniel slowly recalls the evening before and groans. He had a little too much to drink, and Yvette was there, talking to him and then… Daniel groans again.

At the second groan, Yvette wakes and sees Daniel. She lets out a little squeak of embarrassment, covering her face with her hands and then, noting she is still mostly dressed, scrambles away. Daniel laughs slightly, pulling his arm back as he remembers how the shy young lady had become much less shy last night after a few drinks. The laugh makes him wince again as the headache he has acquired makes itself known once more. Rather than suffer through the hangover, Daniel focuses for a moment, casting a Minor Healing on himself.

Crawling out from underneath the wagon, the caravan is slowly waking up. He moves over to the fire, stabbing it to find some coals and adding some of the prepared kindling as he coaches the fire back to life. Asin comes crawling up to him, poking him with one clawed finger till Daniel relents, casting a short Minor Heal on her too.

After breakfast, the wagon rolls out from the town. Asin pokes him again with a claw and jerks her head to the side of the road, and Daniel sighs, joining her as they walk alongside the caravan.

"Yvette." She points to him and Daniel grimaces and nods. She then points to herself and says, "Tevfik."

"Yes, I gathered." Daniel's eyes sparkle slightly, and Asin pokes him again.

"No tell." Asin glares at Daniel and Daniel nods.

"Of course. I won't. Though…" Daniel shifts uncomfortably, looking at the swaying grass and the bright, clear morning. "Well, I might tell Khy'ra myself." He hears Asin sniff at that, shaking her head and Daniel shrugs. "We're not promised to each other, but, well, I'd feel bad. I think."

"Always bad," Asin pronounces before she shrugs, loping back to catch up fully with the wagon. Surprisingly, she takes the front seat with Gabriel without prompting.

The remainder of the day falls into a familiar, mind-numbing routine as the pair sit and watch the ground roll by, occasionally chatting with each other, Gabriel and the passing guards. That evening, Daniel is pulled aside by Iyas to continue his training with the crossbow, making marginal improvements in accuracy and load time.

In the morning, as Daniel wakes up, he is greeted by a notification.

Skill Gained!
Archery: Level 1 (03/100) +3

He cannot help but smile, the troubled sleep from the evening before worth it to finally, finally gain the skill notification. It had taken hours of practice, but at least he finally had the skill. As the noise from around the camp grows, he dismisses the notification. Time to get to work.

***

"What's that?" Daniel frowns, pointing to a growing cloud of dust in the distance hours after they started on the road.

Gabriel frowns, standing up for a brief moment before sitting down unconcernedly. "Plains Nomads. They range in the unsettled areas between the villages in Brad and the border. They are normally peaceful."

Daniel nods, watching as other guards take note of the growing dust cloud and after a moments consideration he picks up and cocks his crossbow, sliding a bolt in. At Gabriel's raised eyebrow Daniel shrugs as he sets the loaded crossbow down next to him in easy reach. Better to be careful and ready than careless and dead.

Daniel's jaw drops slightly as nomads arrive. Clad in a mix of wool and linen with the occasional pieces of unboiled leather thrown in, the nomads sit on small, tough steppe horses with a train of at least two additional horses behind each of them. The nomads each carry a short, recurved bow and a pair of filled quivers. However, it is the fact that the nomads are halflings that truly surprises Daniel, the three-foot tall humanoids chattering excitedly with the wagon masters as their horses easily keep pace with the caravan. The halfling nomad's leader is a woman who animatedly talks with the caravan master before coins are exchanged. The caravan master shouts back to his wagons, calling out the purchased goods while the other nomads spread out to the other wagons, their leader having completed her interactions. They stop by each wagon, speaking briefly with the owner before moving on, only pausing when they find something they'd like to buy.

As one of the halflings rides by him, Daniel's nose wrinkles at the pungent smell that hits him. Gabriel chuckles at Daniel's reaction while Asin gags above them. "Horse fat. They rub it over their body to clean themselves and keep them warm. I hear the nomads think it's bad luck to bathe in rivers and lakes. Something about washing away the good luck."

Daniel coughs, rubbing his nose and is glad as the halflings ride right past their wagon to others further behind. Still, he can't help but watch and admire the experienced horsemen guide their animals with just their feet. Soon enough, the encounter is over, and the nomads break off, riding back into the plains, and the caravan is able to breathe easily.

"Gabriel, is it always this quiet?" Daniel asks as he uncocks his crossbow, returning the bolt to its quiver.

"Of course." The waggoneer laughs.

"Then..." Daniel looks around at the many guards and Adventurers who make up the caravan, and Gabriel laughs again.

"The guards and you Adventurers are a show of force. Bandits and monsters stay away from such a large, well-armed group. If we didn't have you, we'd be attacked more, but with so many guards, it'd take a big or particularly desperate bandit group to attack us," Gabriel explains. "It's why Ios dislikes you Adventurers. He has to pay you to keep the bandits away, but because he pays you, he never gets his money's worth or so he sees it."

Nodding in thanks for the explanation, Daniel sighs and leans back, shading his eyes. It was decent money, but it sure was boring.

***

Days pass, villages blending into one another. It takes them another week to arrive at Silverstone, and there were only three exciting events from Daniel's perspective during that week. The first came a few days after they had left Stolin.

"You, Adventurer! Stay away from my daughter!" shouted the enraged father who waved a finger in front of Daniel's face, drawing the attention of the entire caravan. Behind, an embarrassed Yvettte clutched at her skirts and blushed while Daniel opened his mouth and then shuts it. "You damn Adventurers, sleeping with every young thing. My daughter is too good for your kind!"

"My kind?" Daniel answered stupidly and received another withering stare.

"Adventurers," the father spat to the side, growling. "You think just because you go traveling around, fighting monsters in Dungeons and Leveling up, you're better than the rest of us. Well, you ain't. You keep your hands off my daughter or else I'll deal with you!"

"I'm… I will," Daniel said, changing his mind about apologizing. That evening had been extremely pleasant, and they were both willing adults, even if the young lady was a bit young.

Giving Daniel one last glare, the father stomped away and grabbed his daughter's arm, dragging her off and muttering, "Damn Adventurers! And you, you stupid girl. What will you do if you are pregnant? It's not as if he's going to marry you."

Daniel opened his mouth and closed it, deciding not to explain that he had ensured that no such pregnancy was possible through his Gift. It had required just the barest of touches with his Gift on himself after all. Eyes twinkling, Niko walked up to Daniel, clapped him on the shoulder and guided the youngster away, murmuring, "Right then, let's talk about discretion shall we."

The second incident came two days before they were due to arrive at Silverstone. They had left the plains behind and returned to the forested, rolling hills and cooler temperatures that Brad mostly consisted of. However, it was in one of the forest paths that their first aggressive encounter occurred. A stone bear cub had wandered onto the trail by itself and had been startled by the wagons. Crying out for his mother, the cub had backed off to a corner while the waggoneer had jerked his wagon to a halt. The cub's mother, lingering nearby had rushed out in anger to protect her cub, striking out at the wagon and its guard. Dead after a single swipe, neck snapped and chest torn open, the guard collapsed to the ground as the stone bear mother roared defiance at the unfortunate group.

Standing on his wagon seat, Daniel had swiftly worked to load his crossbow though he was unsure how effective that weapon would be. Iyas jumped down from his perch on top of his wagon, moving quickly to the mother bear without fear. The Ranger spoke to the mother bear, his voice low and calming as he attempted to calm her down. Pulling a bag of berries from his pouch, he offered some to the mother bear before guiding the stone bear and its cub away from the road, a hand on the rough, coarse gray fur. Gabriel breathed a sigh of relief when the animal left and so did Daniel. Knowing one could win did not equal the need to fight, especially against such a powerful monster.

The last event happened the night before they arrived at Silverstone. The three senior Adventurers found the two novices at their cooking fire late in the evening with Niko leading the conversation. "We'll be arriving at Silverstone soon."

"Yes," Daniel said.

"We were thinking, what with you being Adventurers and all. Would you like to see what an Advanced Dungeon is like?" Niko said.

Daniel blinked and looked to Asin, part excited, part scared. As he hesitated, Niko added,

"We won't go past the first level. And we'd share out the earnings in four parts, with both of you taking the fourth. It would be good experience for you two, and it'd be good to have a Healer in the party again, even if it is brief."

Tevfik added his own growling points directly to Asin, working to convince her. She yowled a little, pushing against the other Catkin playfully with her arm before she looked to Daniel and offered a slight nod.

"Well, okay. Only the first level right!" Daniel added and the trio nodded, and Iyas clapped Daniel on the shoulder. Once they had received the two novice adventurer's agreement, the talk turned to what they could expect in the Dungeon they intended to enter, speaking of monsters and dangers as well as the required gear. Most of the gear was common, things that they already owned but some were much more extensive.

No other major incidents occurred before they finally arrived at Silverstone, the arches of the tall buildings that make up the city coming into view.

Daniel smiles as they finally arrive, the city spreading out beneath them in the distance as they crest the hill. Three times the size of Karlak, Silverstone is a major trading hub and the second largest city this side of the country, situated as it is on a meeting point for three major roads and the Arq river that flows from the mountains in the North. Most importantly for Daniel and Asin, it also contains two Advanced Dungeons which contribute a significant portion of wealth to the city.

Like its namesake, Silverstone gleams in the evening sun, as the white walls of the houses and the roofs reflect sunlight and even twinkle ever so slightly to their gaze. The white of the city is not in fact stone but from a unique local clay that when applied helps insulate the houses and gives the city its distinctive look.

As they begin the descent into the city, Daniel smiles and pulls up his character sheet for a moment. They are nearly there!

Name: Daniel Chai
Class: Level 5 Adventurer (6%)
Sub-classes: Level 7 (Miner) (14%)
Human (Male)

Statistics
Life: 215
Stamina: 215
Mana: 160

Attributes
Strength: 20
Agility: 20
Constitution: 28
Intelligence: 16
Willpower: 18
Luck: 13

Skills
Unarmed Combat: Level 3 (17/100)

Clubs: Level 8 (84/100)
Archery: Level 1 (18/100_
Shield: Level 7 (04/100)
Dodge: Level 4 (98/100)
Combat Sense: Level 5 (78/100)
Perception: Level 5 (66/100)
Mining: Level 7 (78/100)
Healing: Level 8 (87/100)
Herb Lore: Level 3 (31/100)
Stealth: Level 2 (14/100)
Cooking: Level 3 (21/100)
Singing: Level 2 (14/100)

Skill Proficiencies
Double Strike
Shield Bash
Mapping (II)

Spells
Minor Healing (I)

Gifts
Martyr's Touch - The caster may heal oneself or others by touch and concentration, sacrificing a portion of his life to do so. Cost varies depending on the extent of the injuries healed.

Chapter 7

"Right then, you lot," the wizened old man barks at the Adventurers, waiting for them to gather before Chip passes around small pouches filled with their pay. The wagons having finally arrived at the city, the caravan master had passed the coin pouches to Chip earlier who now did the distribution. Three smaller pouches for the experienced Adventurers, and two larger pouches for Asin and Daniel for their longer journey. Hefting their pay, the Adventurers slide them into their respective belt pouches and take their dismissal with good grace outside the walls of Silverstone.

"Remember, the Wandering Rooster in two days!" Niko waggles his finger at the two novices who nod quickly. The Rooster was located near the center of town, next to the Adventurer's Guild and nearly directly between the two Dungeons. It was perfectly located and well known to provide high-quality food, comfortable and clean beds and thus cost significantly more than the two novice adventurers could afford. As such, they would be taking rooms closer to the outside walls where cheaper accommodation could be found. While many other inns and buildings lay outside the city's walls, those were often more run down and significantly less comfortable.

The group had already agreed that they would meet in two days to run the Advanced Dungeon. Asin and Daniel first needed to make arrangements for their fetch quest as well as locate and purchase some of the recommended items. It also would allow the two time to tour the city itself, uninjured.

Entrance to the city was a simple affair. The pair had to only showcase their Adventurers seals to be allowed in without paying the entrance fee to the city. Daniel and Asin sighed, wishing that this courtesy was extended to them everywhere else. Of course, this tactic was one that the City of Silverstone had adopted to attract and encourage Adventurers to visit their city over others. After depositing their bags at an inn recommended by Gabriel, the two Adventurers get directions from the innkeeper to the merchant they needed to meet for Max.

As they walk through the city, the two Adventurers unconsciously move closer to one another, unused to the press of humanity. Asin constantly wrinkles her nose, the never-ending stench of civilization pressing on her expanded senses while the constant shouts, rumbling of passing wagons and just the patter of feet assault her ears. Daniel, in turn, finds the sight of so many inhabitants slightly unnerving, and he unconsciously keeps a hand next to his mace, glad to have taken Gabriel's earlier advice to keep the majority of his coins in a pouch hidden inside his shirt.

Most of the inhabitants of Silverstone were dressed like those in Karlak, wearing simple tunics and pants. However, even Daniel noted that many of these tunics were made of higher quality material than those in Karlak. Asin prods Daniel who follows her gaze, and they step into a nearby clothing store to make some quick purchases. They leave in short order, Daniel stalking out with Asin following after, the pair of them growling softly as the proprietor refuses to serve the Catkin. Still, Daniel makes a mental note to go shopping for both himself and Khy'ra before he leaves, preferably in a store that encouraged purchases from a variety of customers.

As he stalks forwards in anger, Asin has to tug on Daniel's arm to get him to go in the right direction as he misses a turn, the little Catkin's tail lashing out behind her. Fortunately, an irate Adventurer who was as broad as Daniel generated a significant amount of space around his body, ensuring that neither Adventurer had to deal with any further casual bumps.

It takes them nearly an hour and a half to find the correct building. Asking for directions often resulted in confusing and sometimes contradictory instructions - the sprawling, winding streets and numerous alleyways meant that the 'fastest' way to a location would differ depending on the particular pedestrian. Finally, at their destination, the pair stare up at the larger warehouse. They tug on the rope situated outside the door, listening to the bell ringing inside as they wait to be let in. They are greeted by a large, tattooed bald man whose skin is nearly as dark as Asin's fur when the door opens. "What?"

Daniel fishes out the letter of introduction, offering it to the man, "We're Adventurers completing a Quest."

The tattooed man grunts, closing the door on the two Adventurers, leaving them on the street. Daniel and Asin look at each other before shrugging their shoulders, setting themselves to wait in the busy street. Ten minutes later the door opens, and the door warden waves them in, looking past them to ensure no others follow. Once he bars the door again, he leads the two Adventurers through the warehouse which surprisingly is sparsely filled with wooden crates shelved with great care. Neither of the Adventurers remarks at the state of the warehouse as neither has ever been in one before, unable to realize that the meticulous and spotless nature of the warehouse was unusual.

At an office in the back, their guide knocks and then opens the door before waving them in. The dark giant steps in soon after the two, taking station behind the pair. Asin automatically shifts, putting herself to the side so that she can watch the larger enforcer, her actions eliciting a narrowing of eyes. Daniel, however, steps forward, his gaze fixed on the merchant before them. At first, he assumes it is a woman due to the delicate features and the makeup, but after a moment he realizes he is mistaken. The gentleman before him has rouged his cheeks, mascaraed his eyes and painted his long, delicate fingers but is still very much a man. Fingers gently glide along the edges of their letter, delicately tracing the words before their owner finally deigns to acknowledge their presence.

"Adventurer's Chai and Asin I presume?" Receiving nods from both he smiles, gesturing for them to take a seat, reaching out to pour glasses of tea for them both. "Come, come. Join me in a drink. Please."

Daniel nods and sits down while Asin shakes her head, preferring to stand and watch the tattooed man. The giant flashes her a grin and is given one in return while the merchant looks at the byplay with a resigned expression.

"I am Leonard Regus. Please, relax and drink. You are guests, honored guests here," Leonard says.

Daniel picks up the glass, sipping at the tea, and is pleasantly surprised at the light and fruity flavor.

"It's good, isn't it? It's a blend we import. If I do say so myself, it is very good. If you want, at the end of this, I'll sell you a bagful. Now, did you just arrive from Karlak?"

"Yes, we did," Daniel answers. Leonard proceeds to ask questions about their journey, disguising his search for information on the condition of the roads in idle chatter. Daniel replies, enjoying the tea and after a while, even Asin relaxes and joins him on sipping the beverage and snacking on the expensive and rare treats that Leonard offers. It is only after fifteen minutes that the conversation turns back to their initial reason for coming, Leonard having pulled sufficient information from the pair to satisfy himself.

"Well, you two have been a delight, a true delight. Your employer's purchases, they are all here. Would you care to inspect them?" Leonard asks, and at their nods of confirmation, he stands and struts to the door to lead them to the appropriate crate. His guard proceeds to pick up the crate from its shelf, placing it on the ground for the two Adventurers to review the items within, checking against the list they were provided. Satisfied, the two nod at Leonard and the guard who proceeds to set the items back on the shelf.

"Now, I understand you need to transport these to Karlak?" Daniel and Asin both nod again and Leonard offers them a regretful smile, "How unfortunate, how unfortunate. There is no caravan leaving for a few weeks, and I must say, it's really sad, but I must say, that one will be traveling to Kyris first. As you know, I'm sure you do, that'll lengthen your trip."

Seeing the crestfallen faces of the duo, Leonard continues, "However, there is a smaller merchant who will be leaving in four days who will be headed to Karlak directly. He usually does not take passengers but if I were to make the introduction…"

"What would you want for this?" Daniel asks bluntly, eyes narrowing. This seemed just a little too convenient.

"Nothing much, nothing at all. Just a little favor that a pair of young, strong Adventurers would find simple to complete," Leonard replies immediately, smiling. "I have a small matter, a small problem, with a competitor and it'd be quite, quite useful if you could perhaps have a word with him. Just a small thing, so very small."

"Guild," Asin speaks up, pointing at him.

"Mmmm… How quaint. How very quaint. Unfortunately, I cannot. I truly cannot speak with the Guild about this. It'd make a private matter public. I really wouldn't want that, and it's such a small favor." Daniel frowns and looks at Asin who shakes her head. Daniel nods back to her and then turns to turn down Leonard again but is cut-off. "Oh, that's so sad. Well, if you do change your mind, do tell me. I could always use your help. Really I could."

The moment he falls silent, the guard has moved up to the pair, indicating for them to leave. Leonard is already heading away, bidding them goodbye and the pair are whisked out in a moment, the goods left in Leonard's hands for now. Standing on the doorstep of the warehouse, the pair frown at each other.

"That was… different," Daniel says and Asin nods, rubbing her nose.

"No trust. Bad," Asin replies and Daniel nods, tapping his mace in thought. Still, the merchant was not going to steal their goods. It would ruin his reputation. After a moment, he shrugs at his partner.

"Well, let's check in with the Guild shall we?" Daniel says, and after getting their directions, the two begin the long hike into the center of town.

***

When they finally arrive at the Guild hours later, after getting lost a few times, the sun has begun to set. The Guild Hall in Silverstone makes both

Adventurers stand in shock as they gaze on the large, three story building that makes up the Hall. It takes up two lots with two separate entrances and a gated yard for training. Late as it is, Adventurers stream out from the entrances at a rapid pace, barely even looking at the two who stand there in shock. Many of the Adventurers split almost immediately to the East and West, headed for the respective Dungeons that lie in those directions.

Asin is the first to get over her shock, prodding her partner to get him moving. Daniel grimaces, hanging his head slightly as he realizes how much of a rube he is looking like and starts walking to the nearest entrance. A few minutes later, both Adventurers hurry back out and enter the other entrance, Daniel flushed with shame. How were they to know that there was a separate entrance for the more senior Adventurers? It wasn't as if there was a sign like the wooden, painted one hanging right outside the door…

In the quest hall, the two Adventurers stare around the large room which is both familiar with its desks and attendants and also so much larger than any other hall they have been to before. The sheer hum of business, of Adventurers and attendants moving in an orderly fashion makes them pause at the doorway again as they attempt to get their bearings. At the loud clearing of a voice behind them, the two scurry to the side and out of the way. Movement to their right catches their attention as they spot an entire room that is set aside for quest notifications through the doorway.

"Wow…" Daniel murmurs and Asin wordlessly agrees with him. Such a difference from Karlak. After a moment more, Daniel shakes his head to clear it and walks to the quest room. They needed to see if there were caravan guard jobs available back to Karlak, preferably earlier. Perhaps the merchant had been wrong?

"Asin Chetan and Daniel Chai? Yes, I've got confirmation of your caravan quest here. Well done. As for your other question, the board is correct. The earliest guard job to Karlak is in two weeks. In fact, we have four jobs from caravans available - though I understand you are looking for the fastest to return to Karlak? That would be Elijah's group in two and a half weeks then," the attendant replies, rubbing at the ink stain on his finger as he scans down the list he has in front of him. Daniel and Asin both sigh, their faint hopes dashed.

"Problem?" the attendant asks and the pair shrug.

"We'd like to sign up for the caravan then. And there's no problem, it's just a little expensive living here," Daniel adds, already thinking of how expensive their inn was. They probably would have to move outside the city gates.

"Don't worry. We've got a lot of work for those of your level. Most of our Adventurers refuse to do the low-level quests we receive, so there's always a backlog." The attendant leans forward, his eyes gleaming. "In fact, if you are willing to get started now, I've got a few quests…"

"Uhh…" Daniel opens his mouth to say no as picking up quests today was not part of the plan. It was getting pretty late, but Asin elbows him aside, nodding firmly to the attendant whose grin widens.

"Perfect! Well, being from Karlak, I have the perfect job for you." The attendant grins, pushing forward a small stack of quest markers. Asin's nose wrinkles as she quickly flicks through them, letting out a low distressed growl.

"I know, I know. Sewers, but these have been piling up so much," the attendant replies and then leans forward conspiringly. "I'll tell you what, if you're willing to take them all, I'll even waive the deposit for all but the top one."

Daniel pushes himself up, and Asin hands him the quest notes which Daniel frowns at, reading them over. Rat extermination. Rat extermination. Pest extermination. Rat extermination. On and on, the sheets continue. "So many…"

"Tell me about it! The guards sweep the sewers every few weeks, but they only ever do the main lines regularly and the rest on rotation," the attendant grumbles, shaking his head. "Of course, that doesn't work if you've got an infestation in your neighborhood."

Asin nods absently, her eyes locked on the bottom of each quest notification, mentally toting up their potential earnings. Her grin widens, coins dancing in her eyes as she considers just how much they could earn.

"I don't know; I mean sewers…" Daniel frowns, glancing over at Asin. The Catkin would suffer even more than he would from the smells.

"All sewer quests receive a token for use at the bathhouse too!" the attendant adds, leaning forward and continuing his hard sell. "It's really a good deal."

Asin nods firmly, pushing the quests forward and shoots a look at Daniel. Daniel grimaces, shaking his head and she growls at him. The young Adventurer grimaces again, eyeing the stack before giving in, "Fine. Can you sort them by location and earnings and what we can finish in one day? We'll then take that pile and a map."

The attendant nods, pulling the stack back and working quickly to do as requested, smiling as he does so. Asin nods happily, already counting their earnings in her head as Daniel mentally grumbles. After they receive their quest papers back along with their requested map and have put down their deposit, the two finally exit the Guild Hall to return home.

"You know, we were supposed to take it easy tomorrow," Daniel grumbles at Asin, waving the stack of quest papers in front of her. "Not go on Quests."

"Money. Good money," Asin says, licking at her paw as she walks along, her tail waving out behind her in happiness.

"Uh huh. You're buying dinner," Daniel states and Asin just nods her head, content to have won that fight.

Chapter 8

Deep in the sewers the next day, Daniel grumbles as he holds up the map to ensure they are in the right spot. Satisfied, he tucks the map away in his leather armor, reaching beyond the glowing mana stone he has attached to it and promising himself he will get his armor cleaned for the umpteenth time that day. He rubs at his nose through the cloth covering, glad that they had taken the time to purchase the enchanted cloths which reduce the smells of the sewer. Otherwise, he knew, he would be regretting this day even more.

For all his grumbling, Daniel still had to admire the extent of the sewers around him. Silverstone's city council had spent the money to hire Dwarven architects and Earth Mages to tunnel the necessary sewers beneath the city, an enlightened act compared to many other smaller cities and towns where waste was allowed to collect on streets or at best, was hauled away late at night by waste carts. The creation of the sewers was an act that was greatly praised by the Healers of the city and one that they continually pushed for in other cities but which was often opposed by the City Guard.

By diverting a small amount of the Arq river through the sewers, the city ensured that the accumulated waste was constantly washed away. However, as the Arq changed in height as the Spring thaw and Autumn rains swept through the land, the sewer tunnels had to be built to accommodate the varying flow rates as well. This ensured that most days the tunnels were not filled to the brim, allowing all manner of monsters and ruffians to use them, creating the reason for opposition by the guard and consistent jobs for the Adventurers.

For Daniel and Asin, they have been in the sewers for two hours already, and they have cleared out the first rat infestation. As natives of the plain, the Devil Rats could grow to enormous sizes if they were able to find sufficient food but both Asin and Daniel had yet to fight one larger than three feet long - not including the tails which were currently stored in Asin's backpack as proof.

Even through the enchanted cloth, the smell of the accumulated waste seeped through, making Daniel take short, careful breaths as he led the way through the carved sewer tunnels. The sewer tunnels started off with a single, large corridor that immediately split into a half dozen smaller lines, each of which then split into smaller tunnels which were fed by lead, clay and metal pipes that ran into the various buildings above. While the initial construction of the lines had been extremely orderly, over time the additions and tearing down of buildings had ensured that new sewer pipes now dotted these smaller corridors which Daniel and Asin traversed. As such, they often had to keep a wary eye above them, skirting around these unorganized additions to the gray stone walls.

As they near the next turn off, Asin runs ahead and grabs Daniel's arm, pulling him to a stop. Daniel frowns, glancing over to the Catkin who has a pair of enchanted cloths covering her face as she raises her other arm with a pair of throwing knives in them. Nodding slightly, Daniel crouches down and waits for her to duck around the corner, her knives flashing forward the moment she does so.

Daniel follows soon after and sees what she heard over the ongoing roar of water, a giant black dung beetle. Her knives burrow into the creature's flesh, sinking deep in and Asin skirts close to the wall to let Daniel rush ahead, lashing out with his mace as he does so. The beetle is soon dispatched, the monster barely more dangerous than a Kobold Chieftain and the pair had dealt with a large number of those. The monster slain, Asin walks forward and extracts her knives and removes an antenna before kicking the body into the stream of sewage.

It was pretty clear to both Adventurers by now why the more experienced Advanced Adventurers of the town declined to complete these quests. The monsters in the sewers were little threat to experienced Adventurers and the quest rewards, while decent for a pair of beginners like themselves, held little attraction to the coin one could make in a Dungeon. Not to forget that they would need to wade through the sewers the entire day.

Grimacing, Daniel moves on. It had taken nearly two hours to make their way this far, and they had at least another half dozen locations to sweep. Still, Daniel pushes on without a word. They had taken the quests; they would complete them. That's what professionals did.

***

Hours later, the two stump into the Guild and to the nearest free attendant's desk. They are immediately rerouted into the Quest room, the main hall devoted to the Dungeon and trading mana stones while Adventurers and attendants hold their breath until they leave. Walking to the Quest room, the pair leave behind looks of disgust and wrinkled noses. Even grumpier than when they started, they finally manage to make their way to the right desk, and Asin drops the bag of rat tails and beetle antennae without prompting. The attendant looks the two over, sniffs and receives the quest notes from Daniel silently, pushing the bag aside without even inspecting the contents.

Minutes later, he has their pay, and their bath tokens, and the pair hurry out, intent on cleaning themselves, their clothing and their armor thoroughly. At the bathhouse, they each hand over their armor and clothing to the attendants to be magically cleansed before they head into their respective sections of the bath houses. Asin, within the female section, is redirected again as she is sent to her own private room due to her fur.

Having washed thoroughly, Daniel relaxes in the hot water pool with his eyes half-closed. Like most other buildings, even the bath house in Silverstone was larger and more grandiose than the one in Karlak. The hot water pool is lined with white marble and situated next to a smaller cold-water pool that is similarly outfitted, sculptures of leaves and vines carved into the lip of the pools. Eyes half-closed, Daniel barely pays attention to the other bathers who move around him till one comes by, letting out a blissful groan as he sinks into the water. Cracking an eye open, he notes the large bruise that covers the man's thigh and hip, and which crawls part-way up his back.

"That looks painful," Daniel says.

"Yes." The man grins, flashing a smile at Daniel as he stretches out in the water and props himself back against the wall. Now that he has more time, Daniel sees that the middle-aged blond man also has numerous other smaller bruises and scratches around his body and a series of older scars. "Life of an Adventurer."

Daniel nods, rubbing his nose before he speaks, "Why don't you get that healed?"

The man laughs, looking at Daniel more closely. "Kid, you don't spend good money on Healers or potions for something this small. Not if you want to save up for any of the good equipment you won't."

Daniel nods slightly, ducking his head down as he realizes that not everyone would have the ability to handle injuries like he did. It had become so routine for himself to fix his or Asin's injuries with minor healing or his Gift that he had forgotten that not everyone had access to that. After a brief pause, Daniel looks up, "I could heal that for you. I know Minor Healing."

The adventurer blinks then laughs, sticking a hand out, "The name's Roy. And I'd be real grateful if you would."

Daniel shakes the man's hand and then while still holding Roy's hand casts his Minor Heal. Roy takes a deep breath when the spell hits him and then relaxes, a wide grin splitting his face as the bruises across his body fade. "Well, isn't that a thing. You actually can Heal. Mighty kind of you."

Daniel shrugs and then blinks as he realizes a number of other Adventurers have come up to him, murmuring about injuries and pointing to them. Daniel twitches, hunkering down a little at the barrage of requests and casts a quick series of spells before claiming to be out of mana. Lips pressed together; Daniel watches the ungrateful Adventurers wade away, the lucky few who were healed laughing at their good fortune and the others quietly grumbling about the Healer who did not have enough mana to heal them all.

"And that's the reason Healer's don't work for free." Laughing, Roy shakes his head at Daniel's pout. "You'll get used to it, kid, you surely will. When you have to fight varmints for everything you get, you start taking whatever you can get for free without thought."

Daniel grunts, unwilling to accept that kind of thinking and regretting opening his mouth at all. At least when he worked at the Clinic in Karlak, he provided a service to those who needed it and who couldn't pay for the services they received. The Adventurers were just cheap and ungrateful.

"So, you're pretty raw for this city. Visiting?" Roy says after watching Daniel mull for a few minutes.

"Yes," Daniel replies, nodding.

"Mmm… and you be having the look of a melee fighter with those muscles," Roy says, eyeballing the broad Adventurer next to him. "What city are you from?"

"Karlak."

"No surprise. Pardon me for asking, but have joined a guild yet?"

"Guild?" Reluctantly drawn in, Daniel leans forward.

"My apologies. I always forget Karlak doesn't have one. No surprise, they rarely bother with Beginner towns, too many flatfoots who will go nowhere there. Adventuring guilds are just a bunch of adventurers who work together in a more formal-like fashion to help each other out," Roy says and his eyes sparkle as he continues. "It just so happens I'm the Vice Guildchair of the Red Roses in this city. Why, we'd be real grateful to have us another Healer."

Daniel blinks, shaking his head slowly. "As I said, I'm just visiting."

"Of course, no rush. As I mentioned, we don't normally recruit Beginners, but you seem like a mighty fine fellow. The guild can provide you some training, some equipment and even have you work with some experienced Adventurers. Nothing like a good old head on their shoulders to keep you safe, you know."

"Okay…" Daniel says, pushing himself up from the pool slightly and smiling back slightly. "Well, I'll think about it."

Roy continues smiling as he nods, "Sure. Sure. Just remember, it's Roy Inverness of the Red

Roses. Just drop my handle, they'll know to expect you."

Standing up fully, Daniel wraps the towel around his body once again and nods jerkily, moving away from the rather pushy Adventurer. He sighs when he finally makes it out, relaxing slightly. Well, that was different.

***

Lip caught between his teeth, Daniel finishes with the letter, setting the quill down with relief. He eyes the sloppy handwriting with distaste, slightly ashamed again about how ugly it looks compared to the flowing script used by scribes. Still, it was what it was. Letting his eyes track over the words again, he wonders if he missed anything.

Dear Khy'ra,

I am writing this letter to you from Silverstone. We have arrived safely and have met with the trader who carries Max's items. Everything looks to be there, but unfortunately, there are no caravans returning to Karlak directly for a few weeks. It seems it will take us even longer to make our way back than we initially planned.

Have you ever been to Silverstone? It is so much larger than Karlak. So much larger than any place I've been to, truth be told. There is so much to see and do! While Asin has been making me do quests with her every day, we still have time to see a little of the city in the evenings. I can't wait to stop owing her money for the armor.

Last night, we went to see a play at a theater. The city is so busy, they even have a dedicated building to host acting troupes all year round! They were doing the Seven Warriors, and it was amazing. They even had a musician playing alongside them. I wish you were here to see it with me.

There is so much to see in this world. I am glad I took this quest even if it took me away ~~from you~~ for a while. Even the quests here are different, and if we ever finish with the sewers, I want us to take a few delivery quests. They are boring and hard work, but it'll give us a chance to see the city more.

We've been invited to test out an Advanced Dungeon with an adventuring party we met on the road. Asin and I are excited to do so, but I must admit, I'm a bit worried. Still, we should be safe with experienced Adventurers around us - they have made it down 6 levels! It's really nice of them to show us around. Don't tell but I think one of the Adventurers is sweet on Asin.

I will see you in a few weeks. By the time you get this letter, it might only be a few days.

Finished reading, Daniel pauses as he wonders how he should sign off. Should he sign off with something other than his name? Perhaps a declaration of love? Yet, neither had said it in person and adding it to the letter seemed wrong. A more formal salutation felt off too. Lips pursed, Daniel stares at the paper, wondering what else to say. Did he even have a right to do so after he slept with another? Did they have that kind of relationship that such things mattered? It didn't seem like it, but then again…

Daniel rubs his temples, making a sudden decision and signing off with only his name and then folding the letter and sealing it. A quick addition of her name and the city and Clinic was enough. Tomorrow, he would hand it to the innkeeper for delivery. Many royal messengers stopped at inns to make some additional coin doing personal deliveries after all, and the innkeeper assured him he had a good relationship with one particular messenger. Lips pursed, Daniel blows the candle out and lays on his bed, troubled thoughts about his relationship keeping him up for a while longer before sleep finally claims him.

Chapter 9

On the second day, the pair finds themselves standing before the Wandering Rooster greeting Iyas and Tevfik. Niko rushes out a few minutes later, still wetting his hair and attempting to get it to stay down as he does so. He grins, waving to the pair as he comes out. Having spent the past few days running the sewers for the Guild, the pair of Adventurers are excited to check out the Advanced Dungeon.

"I see you two brought your bags. Good. And the oil flasks and holy water?" Niko asks, and as the pair nods, he grins. "As we mentioned, we'll take you through the first floor today of Porthos and maybe, depending on how it goes the second floor too. Porthos is better than Aramis for beginners, Aramis being the tougher of the two Dungeons to clear."

The pair nod again at Niko's words, Daniel adjusting his belt to seat his mace better. Niko waits for a moment and looks to his friends before taking the group to the Dungeon entrance. The entrance itself is a simple stone building where a small detachment of guards stand, watching the doors and the Adventurers that enter them.

"Niko, Iyas." The lead guard nods to them, his eyes flicking to Tevfik before moving on to land on Asin and then Daniel. "Additions to your party?"

"Grady. Just showing them the first floor. They're registered Adventurers," Niko replies blithely.

"On your heads. And theirs," Grady says, not even attempting to stop the pair. Why would he after all? Their job was only to stop monsters from coming out and unregistered and foolish children from going in.

Leading the party into the foyer of the dungeon, Daniel blinks as the simple stone room is broken up by a glowing silver portal where a doorway leading to the dungeon itself should be located. Asin beside him lets out a little yowl of surprise and Daniel finds his throat suddenly dry.

"Advanced Dungeons all contain these portals," Iyas replies and claps the pair on the back as he gently guides them forward. "Gave me a real fright too first time I saw one. Don't worry; they work just like the portal stones you're used to in Karlak except that if you're not registered, it sends you directly to the first floor."

"Right then. We're here to give Daniel and Asin a taste of an Advanced dungeon, not kill them. So, Daniel and Asin will be in the center working their long-range weaponry," Niko says. "I'll be in front with Tevfik while Iyas, you'll be scouting. When in the dungeon, my word is law. We'll share the stones and other drops four ways, with Daniel and Asin splitting the fourth share. Any questions?"

Receiving none, Iyas steps forward to the dungeon portal as Daniel hefts his light crossbow and locks a bolt in. As the other party members disappear without a single ripple in the portal, Daniel takes a deep breath and wipes his sweaty palms against his pants before stepping in.

What greets him on the first floor is nothing that Daniel could have imagined. Instead of a small cave, they appear in a single large cavern that seemingly stretches for miles beneath the small ledge that they stand on. Stone walkways are arrayed across the cavern, elevating them thirty to forty feet off the ground immediately, crossing and meeting other walkways that lead higher above to other stone platforms or down to where a rolling white mist forms. Screeches and screams from wheeling birds and other animals echo, along with the slow-grinding of stone as walkways detach from platforms and swing through the air to connect with other platforms or walkways. Light from the mana-saturated stone fills the cave, illuminating the sense-defying scene and giving everything a blue sheen.

Even having had the first floor described to him, Daniel finds himself standing at the entrance in shock as he attempts to grasp the magnitude and absurdity of the dungeon floor. He cannot, even with his elevated vantage point, see the end of the cavern or the ceiling above him, no matter how hard he strains.

Asin next to him lets out a chuff and a low growl of surprise, cursing softly in Catkin as she glares about herself, tail whipping back and forth. At Niko's insistence, she carries a triple batch of throwing knives to make up for the losses that are to be expected through the day. Even now, she clutches a knife in her left hand, the blade sticking out between her fingers.

Having given the pair enough time to view their surroundings, Niko nods to Iyas, signaling him to get a move on. Iyas glides forward, head constantly swiveling to scope out his surroundings, an arrow nocked in his bow. Niko coughs, getting the pair's attention. "Right, come along then. The monsters aren't going to kill themselves."

Walking together, the Adventurers scan their surroundings searching for threats. After a moment, Asin prods Daniel and points to Niko. Daniel frowns and not seeing what she does, raises an eyebrow. She lets out a chuff, her tailing having returned to its usual lazy waving as she points to her eyes and then up. Daniel slowly nods, realization coming as he begins to look upwards for threats. It is not a moment too soon as Niko grunts out, "Trouble."

Daniel spots the Imps a moment later, a dozen scaled, warty figures gliding down with their bat-like wings spread out behind them. The monsters are mostly black with shades of red highlighting claws, pointed ears, and sharp, needle-like teeth. Snapping his crossbow to his shoulder, Daniel waits for the monsters to come near him. At the speed that they are approaching, he will only have one good shot.

Depressing the trigger slowly and gently, Daniel remembers to shoot for where the imp will be and not where it is. The bolt flies true when it leaves, catching an imp in its chest and knocking the monster away. Ahead of him Niko crouches, eyes tracking the pair of Imps that close on him before he draws his sword. Activating a Skill, the swordsman's strike moves so fast, the air in front is compressed into a thin line along the edge of the blade, sending a wave of compressed and super-sharp air tearing into the Imps who dare to attack him. Wings and bodies shredded, the Imps smash into the walkway, what's left of their wings feebly beating against the ground.

"That's how you do it!" Niko calls out as he darts forward to thrust his sword into the Imps bodies. "Otherwise the Mana stones get lost!"

Daniel has no time to answer, working on cranking his crossbow while Asin stands next to him, throwing her knives at the monsters that rush the group. Tevfik keeps close to the two, stepping forwards to strike with his sword when an Imp comes too close, crippling the wing before he stomps on the creature's neck. Ahead of them, Iyas has turned around and sent a pair of arrows into the sky, each arrow bringing a monster down.

Without a word, Asin grabs hold of Daniel and pulls him down, a ball of conjured fire flashing past where his head was. Eyes wide, Daniel drops the bolt and has to scramble for it on the ground even as Tevfik catches another fireball on his shield, enchanted runes flaring to life as they provide additional protection against the heat. Asin is on her knees, charging another blade and sending it straight into a throat, the blade piercing the creature's open mouth. The Imp lets out a little gurgle, falling to the ground and as Daniel finally looks up, bolt seated, he finds the wave wiped.

Niko quickly moves around the dissipated bodies, picking up the mana stones and pocketing them while Iyas keeps a further eye out. "Not bad, eight stones and two imp teeth. Remember, shoot when they are over the walkways."

Asin hops over to grab a pair of her blades that fell on the path while Daniel grimaces, realizing how little he did in that fight. The entire battle had happened so fast!

"Iyas," Niko calls out and Iyas moves on, continuing to lead the party deeper into the dungeon.

***

The following hours have opened the two young Adventurers' eyes to the level gap between them and the experienced Adventurers they party with. Each attack consists of at least a dozen Imps, often more and yet the party of three cut through the monsters with frightening ease. The fighters never waste any motion, each attack bringing an Imp to the ground to be finished. Skills are used sparingly and with precision, often triggered to take down multiple monsters at a time.

As impressive as their combat skills are, it is their teamwork that makes Daniel and Asin truly jealous. The group rarely speaks, and when they do, it is normally to order Daniel and Asin around. Otherwise, the well-oiled party work together smoothly, never targeting the same monster nor leaving gaps in their defenses as they fight.

"Asin, Daniel, come!" Iyas calls out. Daniel looks up, pushing away his thoughts about the differences in strength and hurries forward. Iyas waves them forward to where a new walkway starts, carefully brushing aside the dirt to reveal a pressure tile.

"See it? Right, watch this." Glancing back to ensure the two are on the platform, Iyas backs off as well and throws a small pouch filled with dirt onto the tile. The weight is enough to depress the tile, and the entire walkway immediately tilts to the side, spinning halfway and tipping dirt and debris into the air before it rotates back.

"Shit!" Daniel shouts, his eyes wide as he imagines what would have happened to any Adventurer unlucky enough to be caught by that.

"Yes. Feather Fall enchantments are quite popular." Iyas chuckles, waiting for the groaning walkway to right itself. When the walkway rights itself, he continues speaking. "See how the dirt, especially on this side, is slightly higher? Comes from the repeated tipping. You got to watch out for that."

Niko waits for the lesson to be over before he clears his throat, waving back to the platform. "Good time to have lunch."

Receiving confirming nods, Iyas elects to be on the first watch while the others eat. Almost immediately, Tevfik and Asin move to a corner of the platform, their tails curling around each other as they growl softly.

"So, what do you think?"

Daniel startles slightly, blinking up at Niko guiltily as he turns away from watching the two lovers. "Ummm…. none of my business."

"Not them, the dungeon!" Eyes twinkling, Niko pokes Daniel who flushes.

"Oh! Of course, that's what you meant." Daniel pushes thoughts of getting berated by Elder Chetan aside as he replies to Niko. "It's amazing. I never thought it'd be so big. And the monsters, they aren't that much tougher than Kobolds, but there's so many of them! And those burns sting!" Daniel rubs at his arm, remembering how Tevfik was unable to catch a fireball completely on his shield, splashing Daniel with just a touch of the explosion.

"It's why we chose Porthos," Niko says. "The Imps aren't that strong, and so long as we keep them focused on us, you two should be pretty safe. Especially with your healing abilities. Aramis on the other hand - well, the Kulark are much harder to fight. They can slither faster than you'd think and their scales are extremely hard. Worst, because they're sentient, they'll target you and Asin first."

Daniel nods at that, looking out at the vista spread before them. In the distance, he thinks he can spot another pair of Adventuring groups, but the level is so large and the pathways so numerous that meeting another team would require significant effort and planning. Running a hand through his black hair, Daniel lets out a sigh.

"Thinking about how far you have to go?" Niko enquires as he spots Tevfik get up with Asin to relieve Iyas.

"A bit."

Niko just nods at that, standing up to have a chat with Iyas. A small smile tugs at the corner of

Niko's lips as he stands, a smile that is hidden from Daniel as he crosses over to his friend to plan the rest of the day.

***

"Right then, you see the big Imp there? That's the Overseer - they are evolved Imps, and while they can't fly, they are a lot bigger and stronger. They can cast Fire Dart too which sends smaller but more numerous fire arrows," Niko explains as he points out the floor champion they have located after hours of trekking through the dungeon. "Iyas and Asin will deal with his minions. I will fight the Overseer directly while Daniel will focus on killing any Imps Iyas and Asin bring down. Tevfik is on guard duty with his shield."

After a series of nods, Daniel pulls his shield off his back for the first time that day, sliding it over his arm. He quickly secures his crossbow to his body with a strap on his leg before hefting it in his other arm, ready to be dropped at a moment's notice. Daniel plans to shoot the single loaded bolt then immediately drop it for his mace. As he finishes his preparations, Tevfik points to Daniel's shield. "Pour the holy water on it."

Preparations complete, the party moves forward quickly at a light jog. There is no way to surprise the Overseer, so it is better to get to the monster quickly before it can call for more reinforcements.

Halfway to the Overseer on the final walkway, Iyas pulls to a stop and begins shooting at the Imps that have begun to converge on them. Asin skids to a stop next to him, throwing knives held out before her while Niko sprints the last few yards. Daniel spots that not all the Imps have left the Overseer's side and brings his crossbow to bear, shooting an Imp that attempts to block Niko's path out of his way.

The next few minutes are a blur for Daniel as he runs from downed Imp to downed Imp, all the time trying to keep an eye out for errant fireballs. Iyas provides cover fire for Daniel without a break, his hands blurring as he fires.

As Imps dart forward to strike at Daniel in ever increasing numbers, Tevfik raises his head to the ceiling and lets out a snarl that raises the hairs on the back of Daniel's neck and arms. He freezes for a brief moment, the primordial part of his mind recalling other beasts before he can push past it. The Imps, the targets of the Skill, are not as lucky and all freeze for a few minutes, struck by fear, and this allows the ranged attackers to attack freely. Iyas does not waste the opportunity, his hands glowing as he constantly pulls on the bow and fires arrows made of green energy at the Imps. Asin spins around and throws her knives as well, each shot targeted at a different Imp.

Daniel is left to run back and forth, swatting at Imps and stomping on them when he can. As the Imps push the fear aside, they screech and divert their attention to attack the greater danger, all of them launching themselves at Tevfik now. Asin scoots to the side, throwing a last dagger before pulling out the enchanted oil flask. She watches, occasionally striking down an Imp that comes too close before snarling out in Catkin as throwing the flask into the air after triggering the enchantment. The flask shatters, sending flaming oil around and catching many of the Imps in the blast radius. Tevfik, warned beforehand is crouched behind his enchanted shield, the explosion giving him a momentary respite.

Behind them, Daniel spots Niko cutting upwards with his sword, the Skill triggering to pick up the Overseer from the ground. Even as the creature begins to fall, Niko cries out and lunges forward, spearing the monster with his blade and then twisting in his hips to tear the wound wide open, ending the monster.

Daniel has no more time to watch as he catches a fireball on his shield from a downed Imp, the backdraft of heat singeing hair and eyebrows. He pushes forward, dropping his shield onto the creature's body and crushing it before it can breathe again, using his lowered body to allow him to swipe at another Imp.

A few minutes of intense battle later, the bodies of the Imps fade away in motes of blue light while the Adventurers catch their breath. Asin rubs ointment into her ear where an Imp caught her as it flew past, and Niko favors his leg while the others check over other minor injuries. Once he is able to, Daniel moves among the group and casts his spells, starting with Niko who proceeds to gather their loot. As he heals them, he receives murmured thanks, Iyas shooting Tevfik a knowing glance after being healed.

***

Later that evening in the Wandering Rooster, Niko drops a pouch onto the table where the other party members have been waiting, drinking.

"Not too bad a haul for the first floor," Niko says. "Split four ways, that's 1 Gold, 2 Silver and 2 Copper each. As requested, we didn't change the stones that fit your needs, Daniel, and split them into your pile instead as part of your share." He then drops two Copper coins on the table. "Oh, and there's this leftover. Tip?"

He gets nods from his party members of course and at the raised eyebrow from Daniel to whom he explains, "We just add it to the waitress tips when it comes up like this."

"Oh..." Daniel nods in agreement, the mystery of the good service explained. While Daniel is getting the explanation, Asin has pulled the pouch aside and deposited the contents out, quickly shifting the stones to the side before counting the remaining coins. Her ears wilt slightly at how much it has reduced, especially as they were still two stones short!

"So, you leveled up eh?" Iyas says, returning to their prior conversation.

"Yes! Amazing that it happened with just one trip." Daniel nods quickly.

"Mmm... There were a lot of monsters today. It's another reason we chose Porthos," Niko adds.

"What Skill are you going to choose?" Niko asks, curiously. "Are you going to get another Healing Spell?"

Asin tilts her head to Daniel too, nose wrinkling as she considers what her friend will do. More healing would be nice, though Daniel was only a moderately good fighter right now.

"Maybe…" Daniel trails off, not having thought too deeply about his choices yet.

"No! Don't waste your Skill Up on that. You can learn Spells with training," Iyas declares, and Daniel grimaces.

"I wish. The cost alone of renting a Healer's time to train me…" Daniel shakes his head. "It's impossible, at least for me."

"That's why you should join our Guild!" Iyas blurts out and then yelps, rubbing at his foot and glaring at Niko.

"Guild?"

"Yes, we're all part of the Green Robin," Niko replies, tapping at the badge that is situated on each of their cloaks. Daniel blinks, having noticed it before but not recognizing its significance. He had thought it was just a party badge - after all, even Beginner Adventurers in Karlak had done it. "What do you think? Interested? You and Asin could run Advanced dungeons all year long with different parties, increasing levels at a higher rate. And as a Guild member, the Guild would help locate and pay for your lessons just like it does for Mages."

Daniel frowns and then his eyes narrow slightly before he looks between the three experienced Adventurers. His voice laced with suspicion; he says, "You invited us because you wanted us to join your Guild didn't you?"

"Well, partly. We did want to show you around though, we like you guys," Niko hastily adds.

"Why?" Asin says, her tail unwrapped from Tevfik and now sticking out beneath her chair straight down.

"Well, we…"

"Why?" Asin repeats.

"Daniel's a healer. Is that what you want to hear? Healers who aren't priests are really, really rare. And most priests are a pain to work with - their abilities come from their Faith, so the better the Priest, the more Faithful they are to their God. We partied up with a Priest before from Mohin who would never work on the Fifth Day. So yeah, we want, the Guild wants, any healers they can find," Niko replies exasperatedly.

Daniel looks to Iyas who just offers a short nod while Tevfik growls softly to Asin. She lets out a low snarl in return, moving her hand away from his before she stands, stalking out. Daniel looks between the three before he stands up and rushes out after his friend, Niko calling out quickly, "Think about it!"

As the door shuts, Daniel glimpses Niko berating Iyas for bringing up the Guild so abruptly, disrupting his plans. Daniel has no time to watch though as he hurries after his friend.

"Asin…"

She stalks onwards, not saying a word, tail lashing out side to side behind her as her shoulders hunch. Pedestrians scramble to get out of the short Catkin's way, the glower and array of knives a clear warning to all.

"I didn't know. I mean, there was this other guy who asked me to join his Guild, but I didn't know…" Daniel blathers on, filling the silence. "I mean, they don't even know about my Gift, and they want me this badly. I wonder what they'd be like if they knew. I guess it's good the other Adventurers didn't, but I know Liev mentioned it might be an issue…"

Asin lets out a little growl, and Daniel shuts up, her stalking carrying them through the city streets quickly. After a time, she says softly, "Tevfik no like me. Just you."

"I don't think that's true, Asin," Daniel adds quickly. "I mean, he's always watching you…"

"Idiot," Asin says, and for a moment Daniel wonders who she means. He opens his mouth to ask and then remembering her growl, shuts up, finishing the walk back to their inn in silence.

Chapter 10

"I'm not complaining about being out of the sewers, Asin, but did we have to take quests so far away?" Trudging out of the city, Daniel grumbles as he hefts his backpack. They had only been in Silverstone for a few days, as it stood, and now they had left it again on another quest. This one involved a visit to a nearby village to help the farmers fight off attacking vermin while they completed their harvesting.

It was not a glamorous job, but it certainly paid well as the farmers needed to attract the Adventurers away from the Dungeons. Luckily, with the Skills that most farmers gained, they were able to manage and see to large tracts of land, allowing them to handle the expense. Truthfully, from Asin's point of view, the most important aspect of the quest was for once not the pay but that it got the pair out of Silverstone and away from that traitorous, two-faced Catkin.

Seeing that his partner has decided to ignore him, Daniel glances over to the side and spots a familiar face from the Guild Hall. Not seeing a guild badge on the group, Daniel diverts himself slightly to say hi.

"Morning there!" Daniel calls out, and the group of Adventurers turns to him. The middle-aged, slightly potbellied mace wielder he spotted eyes Daniel for a moment before grinning and waving to Daniel.

"You're the youngsters from Karlak," the older gentlemen replies, smiling.

"Yes. I'm Daniel."

"Lin. This is Ingrid and Jorge," Lin indicates his older companions, a redhead in an old but well-maintained suit of chainmail and a darker skinned, spear-wielding companion in turn. "You heading to Ilquin too?"

"That's right. The quest pays very well," Daniel says.

"Definitely. It's why we do it. I'm impressed you managed three days in the sewers though. Most groups give up after the first."

Ingrid shudders at the mention of the sewers and Daniel finds himself rubbing his nose, the smell coming back to him once again. He is not surprised that the group knows of their exploits, Adventurers had a tendency to gossip worse than housewives. After all, learning as much as you could about the monsters and levels you would face could keep an Adventurer alive.

"Which Dungeon do you run otherwise?" Daniel asks, curiosity filling his voice.

"None," Jorge answers for the group and seeing Daniel's surprised look, he continues. "We're questors."

"Huh?"

"We don't run Dungeons anymore, Daniel. We focus on quests only," Ingrid quickly explains, her voice surprisingly high pitched for such a rough looking woman. "We gave up on all of that dangerous delving a while ago. That's what questors are - Adventurers who only do quests."

"Oh…" Daniel falls silent then frowns. "But we were told there weren't enough quests being taken up."

"Not at your level," Lin chuckles. "Just because we're retired doesn't mean we want to do fetch quests or the sewer."

"Is this dangerous then?" Daniel frowns, recalling that Asin had appeared at his door this morning with the quest already taken.

"No, not really. It's a longer quest since it takes a few days for the harvest to be brought in, but overall, it's a pretty easy quest. The biggest danger is the Spotted Deer which are running, and those are easy enough to scare away. At least for us Adventurers," Lin pronounces, and Daniel nods slowly. "Ever met the deer before?"

"No."

"Har, alright then. Come on; I'll tell you about them and the quest…"

***

"Smell good," Asin says, walking over to peer at the meal the experienced Adventurers are making. Lin laughs, waving her to take a seat as he flips the pan, sending the thin slices of meat into the air before catching them.

"That's quite a compliment coming from Asin," Daniel says, shaking his head as he sees how fast the group has set up their sleeping area. He and Asin had just finished setting up their own camp and were in the middle of gathering wood, and these three were already cooking.

"Join us then," Jorge says as he brings back a pot of water which he hangs over the fire. The moment it is hung, he moves to the waiting vegetables which he begins to throw in. "Lin always brings more than enough."

"You'd pack more too if you ever got stuck in a snowstorm on Pare Peak like I did. Ended up chewing on our leather vests just to eat something!" Lin replies, a slight smile twisting his face. "Of course, that's when I learned that Derin Lizard brains are quite good."

"Don't corrupt the kids, Lin," Ingrid says, dropping her bundle of wood. "Right, if you add your pile to ours, we'll have more than enough for tonight."

Asin nods with alacrity, leaving Daniel behind as she accedes to the invitation. After a brief questioning, Daniel moves away too to bring along the meat he was to cook and watches as Ingrid slices and spices the meat with deft strokes. Asin prods at the spice, sniffing at the spices with interest as she deposits the wood.

"Why were you on Pare Peak?" Daniel says once he is situated comfortably and out of the way of the smoke from the fire.

"A quest of course. This young nobleman wanted an escort to find the Yeti." Lin rolls his eyes, "Hired two whole parties for three weeks and paid good coin for it. We ended up stuck there for two months when we were snowed in. Luckily, the quest was paid by the day. I bought a pair of enchanted swords from that quest." Lin smiles, dark eyes remembering past glories before he sighs, "Those broke half-a-year later fighting a stone golem."

Putting the cooked meat aside, Lin accepts the newly seasoned slices onto his pan while Ingrid says, "Two swords! I used to have a set of fully enchanted plate. Had to sell it to pay for all the healing potions we needed after a bad delve when we needed to heal Quinn, our Mage. Healers are a damn scam."

"You're telling me. I ended up being a questor because I needed to sell off all my equipment just to cover the bill to regenerate my foot," Jorge adds, shaking his head. "Though I guess I could thank him too."

"Definitely thank him, if that's why you became a questor," Lin follows up before waving them closer to him. "Right, the first batch is ready, get your plates."

The group stops grousing for a time as they work through the bread and meat that is provided, Lin occasionally returning to the pot to stir and taste the vegetable soup. As everyone begins to finish up, Asin turns to regard the experienced Adventurers, "Why questors?"

Lin pauses, spoon halfway to his lips before he lowers it. Jorge sighs, rubbing at his beard when Asin asks her questions.

"You normally don't ask that. It's considered rude," Lin said.

"Why?" Asin prods, scratching at her ear as her tail waves lazily.

"Most other Adventurers consider us failures," Ingrid explains. "In fact, most won't even speak with us."

As Asin opens her mouth to ask why again, Daniel kicks her in the foot. She glares at him but says nothing, turning back to her soup. Lin watches the unsubtle interaction, and his lips twist in amusement before he says, "I was a guild leader once. Just a small one, we only had about forty members. Then we had a few bad months, a few of our parties were lost, and others were poached. We eventually disbanded and then, well, I hadn't done that much delving since I became a guild leader, and I realized I wasn't interested anymore. So, I just started doing quests."

"I couldn't get past the eighth floor no matter what I tried," Jorge speaks up, looking at his bowl of soup as he adds his own story. "I was always the one making the mistakes, always the one holding the team back. They eventually decided to cut me loose after I lost my foot and I couldn't find another team to join permanently. I worked quests when I didn't have a group or in-between delves and eventually, well, I just stopped trying."

Asin and Daniel look to Ingrid whose lips purse before she says, "No." Disappointed, the pair turns back to their meal. Later, when Ingrid has left, Jorge murmurs to the pair as they leave, "She lost her party in a bad delve. Never tried again."

Daniel nods in thanks and invites them over for breakfast the next day in turn. As he walks back, he cannot help but think that being an

Adventurer has more paths than the single one that he initially imagined and that for many, those paths ended in heartache.

***

True to Lin's prediction, the next few days pass without incident. Watching from his assigned spot, Daniel wipes rain away from his eyes before scanning the surroundings again, stopping on the farmers as they finish up the latest field. Barely a dozen in number, the workers had cleared three fields today just by themselves, even while working in the pouring rain. In fact, the greatest delay was in storage as carts struggled along the muddy roads to deliver the produce to the warehouses.

Once again, Daniel smiles as he watches the farmers work. He was always amazed at how so few Farmers can produce such a large harvest - though realistically, it is no different than how experienced Miners can churn out significantly more ore than beginners. If not for the need to continually train the next generation of workers, youngsters like him would never be given a significant role in mining operations.

"Deer," Asin says, her hood pulled tight over her head as rivulets of water drip down around her. As she speaks, she points, and Daniel wrenches his gaze away. In the distance, he sees the Spotted Deer herd run downwind of them, each motion a thing of beauty. They glide across the ground but veer off suddenly as the smell of old and rotten blood carries its way to them. Daniel relaxes and then reaches for his water bottle, feeling the lukewarm water wet his throat.

"So… this is the last day it seems. We'll probably even be able to get back before the evening falls if we hurry," Daniel says.

"Mmmm…" Asin purrs.

"What I'm saying is that we could enjoy a soft bed, warm water, and a hot meal if we decide to." Daniel tries again as he pulls his own cloak tighter, feeling the chill from the rain carry to his bones.

Again, all Asin does is purr.

"Are we going back tonight?" Daniel cries out exasperatedly, and Asin lets out a chuckle, looking up at him from where she crouches, her tail waving lazily in amusement.

"Yes."

"Good." Daniel nods firmly, stretching. "So, you're good then?"

Asin nods and then shrugs after a moment. "Foolish. Over now."

"I still think Tevfik liked you for yourself you know," Daniel adds, but seeing the glare Asin shoots him, he then shuts up. Soon enough, the work is done, and Daniel heads over to wish goodbye to the other Adventuring parties and the Farmers before the pair head back to the city. Asin pauses for a moment, staring back to Daniel before she flashes him a grin and takes off, loping forward at speed through the mud, Daniel growling softly as he hurries to keep up with her. Damn cat.

***

"Daniel!" Niko waves to the youngster as he walks in, cold and grumpy at having lost the race back. Asin had out-paced him very quickly and never seemed to look back, so all that Daniel could do was follow after her, alternately jogging and running. Having finally made it back to the inn, Daniel only wants to rest in his room and so ignores Niko, heading upstairs.

He is pulled short by Niko's hand on his arm halfway up the stairs, the older swordsman looking serious. "Daniel, I just need a moment. Please."

Daniel frowns and then nods, recalling how the other Adventurers had helped them. He owed Niko at least the courtesy of listening to him. In the dining hall, Daniel quickly orders some mulled wine to warm his body before he turns to Niko, waiting for him to speak.

"I know you're upset we hid our intentions from you. I just wanted to explain it to you," Niko said. "You see, well, finding an unaffiliated healer is incredible. Even someone who only has Minor Healing can make a difference in a party's earnings over the long-term, and if you ever learned more powerful spells, you could make a major difference on a day-to-day basis.

"Few parties ever advance beyond an Advanced Dungeon without a healer in the party. Even including the priests though, there just never are enough of them to go around. Finding a healer that's unaffiliated is a big thing for a small guild like ours."

"I've figured that out," Daniel answers grumpily.

"I still think you should join a guild, even if it's not ours. There's no reason for you to be working a dungeon like Karlak, earning a few silver every run when you could be in a real dungeon. With a guild's help, they could outfit you with proper equipment and ensure you got the right training."

"Out of the goodness of their hearts?"

"Of course not. You're an investment, and they'd expect you to use your skills for the good of the guild. But it's nothing more than what you offered to do in the bath house," Niko points out.

"Oh, you found out about that eh?" Daniel grimaces and Niko nods.

"And I know what you did for the travelers too. You'd just be using your gifts for other Adventurers instead."

"You'd treat me like a Healer though."

"That's what you are. We'll protect you and make sure nothing happens to you. The worst thing you can do is have your Healer killed!" Niko adds, shaking his head.

"Right, right," Daniel sighs and drinks down his wine, standing up. "Thank you for that, Niko. I'll… think about it."

Niko nods, disappointed. As he stands, he offers Daniel a patch from his guild, saying, "If you change your mind, just show this at the reception of our guild hall and state my name. I'll leave word to keep an eye out for you. And Asin."

Daniel nods again, putting the patch away in his pouch as he heads up the stairs. A part of him can see the advantages, the way that joining a guild could make up for his Gift and meet his dreams.

However, it meant he would be treated as a precious commodity, a healer that could never be injured. No longer would he be allowed to risk himself in dungeons that might be a little too difficult for him or fighting bosses. Daniel would be a healer, and healers never fought in the front.

Still, this offer would let him make up for lost time. Daniel knew he was old for a beginner Adventurer, old to have just started on this journey. While Levels and experience could help stave off the effects of time, time still always won.

Lying in bed, Daniel stares at the wooden boards that make up the ceiling, his thoughts going in circles.

Chapter 11

"No, it's left," Daniel insists, glaring at Asin. "Who's the one with the Mapping skill?"

Asin glares and points down to the left before adding, "Been there."

"I know we have, but the instructions lead us down there. We must have missed something!" Daniel reiterates, and Asin shakes her head firmly.

"No miss. Nothing there. Right."

"Asin!" Daniel growls again, and Asin sniffs, holding up a finger. When Daniel subsides, the Catkin continues.

"Try once."

"Aaargh! Fine." Huffing in defeat, Daniel shifts the pack he carries once more. When he does so, the scratching coming from within the backpack makes him shiver again. Asin looks over as well, her hearing picking up the noise. "Not doing this again."

Asin nods firmly, shuddering. Delivery quests within the city itself were rare – after all, there were numerous cheaper options. When this quest came up, Daniel had snatched it up quickly as a way to see more of the city. How were they to know that the special delivery was for a box of Umben Beetles.

Umben Beetles were flesh-eating monsters that would swarm the nearest host, burrowing into the flesh and laying eggs where more of their kind would grow, eventually crippling and killing its host. When that happened, the Umben Beetles would exit and find a new host, continuing the cycle. They were also considered a noble delicacy, the creatures carefully cultivated across numerous hosts for the exotic, layered flavors their hosts imparted on the Beetles.

Daniel is brought out of his thoughts by a gloating Asin who points to where the sign of a crossed fork and lamp are painted above the restaurant's name 'The Fork & Lamp' are painted. Daniel looks once more at the directions and growls, "It says left!"

Before Asin can answer an angry, balding man throws the door open, shouting, "You're late!"

"The directions we were given were wrong!" snaps Daniel and the man snarls.

"I don't care about your damn excuses. Filthy, money grubbing Adventurers. I should complain to your Guild!" snaps the man, reaching out to grab the box from Daniel. Daniel almost holds it back before remembering he wants the box off his back as soon as possible and hands it over. Without another word, the bald man stomps back into his restaurant, already screaming at his employees.

"I hate city people," growls Daniel and Asin wrinkles her nose, eyeing the restaurant. After a moment she shakes her head, gesturing for Daniel to lead the way back. They were unlikely to be served well if they went in to dine right now, which was a shame in Asin's view. After all, the Fork & Lamp was considered one of the premier restaurants in the city. Sighing to herself, Asin follows behind Daniel as they head back to the Guild Hall.

***

"How about this one?" Daniel asks, holding up a quest note asking for guards. Asin reads over the note, shaking her head and points to the pay rate. Two silver for each Adventurer was very poor. Instead, she taps on another and Daniel reads it aloud, frowning. "Alchemist looking for participants in their experiments. Must have high Constitution."

Asin nods firmly, and Daniel eyes her doubtfully. She lets out a huff and points to Daniel before growling softly, "Heal."

"Oh! Oh…." Daniel frowns, tapping his fingers. Well, it was true that they could probably survive the experiments with his healing and Gift but still… At Asin's insistent pointing at the bottom of the quest that indicated the rewards which were for each potion they decided to take, he finally relents. "Fine, fine."

Grinning, Asin bounces off with the quest marker to get it assigned to them while Daniel continues to peruse the rather extensive list of quests.

***

"A Catkin!" The short human grins, pulling on Asin's arm as he leads her to a chair. "This should be…" Daniel and Asin wait, the man turning after a time and spotting the young Adventurer and waving him to a seat too.

"So, let's see…" Muttering to himself, the man tugs at his ear as he walks between rows of potions. Each is marked with tape and a series of numbers and letters. Finally, the human picks and brings across two pinkish red vials. "Take this and drink when I say so."

Pulling a notepad from a nearby seat, the Alchemist jots a series of words down before looking up at the patiently waiting pair. "Well, go on then!"

Asin chuffs out, her tail flicking in irritation before she sniffs at the potion again. It didn't smell wrong at least. Downing it quickly before she can think of a reason not to, she turns to look at Daniel who is more gingerly sipping on the concoction, a part of his mind holding his Gift ready just-in-case. The Alchemist peers at the pair, watching them for adverse reactions.

Nothing happens for a few minutes before the Alchemist nods, smiling. "Good, good… why is that purple?"

Daniel blinks, and Asin holds her nose, skirting away from the Adventurer before suddenly realizing that her stomach needed to release some gas too. Letting out a loud burp, she watches the cloud of purple smoke escape her mouth.

"Well, that's different," mutters the Alchemist, making notes. He grabs a knife, swinging it towards Asin who skirts back. When no one moves to take it, he waggles the knife again. "Well, go on and cut yourself. Do I have to tell you everything?"

"Yes," Daniel says bitingly, taking the knife carefully from the Alchemist. He rolls his sleeve up before gently nicking his arm. Blood wells up as Daniel grunts, waiting to see what might happen.

"Hmmm… No residual regeneration. Okay," the Alchemist mutters and points to Asin. "You."

Asin nods, testing the blade on her own arm as well and finding no change. After a moment, the Alchemist comes back with more of the same potion, nodding for them to drink. "One at a time!" he barks when he notes Daniel about to drink as well.

Again, he watches the young Catkin, keeping an eye on her wound as he tugs on his ear in thought. The wound heals slowly, purple smoke pouring from the wound even as Asin finds herself gassy again.

"1, 2, 3, 4… and that's it. Now, you." The Alchemist points to Daniel before they repeat the procedure. When they are finally done and healed, the Alchemist sniffs, scribbling in his notes. After a time of being ignored, Daniel clears his throat.

"How many more?"

"Hmmm?"

"How many more potions are we testing?"

"Oh, four more with six variations each," the Alchemist answers absently, waving to them to be quiet.

Daniel subsides, looking at Asin who lets out another purple burp. Well, maybe it wouldn't be that bad.

***

"Yes! That's perfect!" the Alchemist shouts jubilantly while Asin growls, batting at the swarm of flies and other flying bugs that surround her.

"It's supposed to do that?" Daniel says, horrified.

"Of course! It's a potion of insect attraction," the Alchemist says, puzzled at how Daniel could not understand something so simple. "Your turn!"

***

"That's not supposed to happen…."

"YOU THINK!" Daniel shouts, clutching at the table as he floats up in the air. As suddenly as he lost the ability for gravity to affect him, he finds himself crashing into the ground again. Holding his arm which he landed awkwardly on, Daniel glares at the Alchemist.

"I wonder what a double-dose would do…?"

***

"Why'd you drink that? That's not supposed to be drunk."

"Uaarggh." Asin would have shouted at the Alchemist, but she was currently hunched over the bucket, throwing up the foul-smelling liquid.

"Application only. Says so right on the… oh, right. Label. My fault!"

"Uaarggh."

***

"This one works very well," Daniel says, grinning as he lifts the table with one hand.

"No, it doesn't," mutters the Alchemist, shaking his head.

"What do you mean? I'm so strong," Daniel says.

"It's not a strength potion. It's a…."

"A..?

"Skin exfoliator. It's supposed to make your skin shine."

"Why'd you make Asin drink it too?" Daniel asks, puzzled as he lets the table down. It's not as if the Catkin had much skin to exfoliate.

"Science!"

***

"Now remember, write down any symptoms you experience over the next few days," the Alchemists says, pressing sheets of paper into the Adventurers' hands. Daniel and Asin both nod dumbly, eyes glazed with the sheer variety of things that have happened to them this day. When they finally escape, the pair look at each other and then find themselves hurrying along down the road, their fast walk turning into a run by the end of the street.

Never again!

***

Another series of complaints had generated a series of quests, and the pair were in the dark again, crawling through the sewers. In truth, after their recent quests, these sewers were quite relaxing. Straightforward and easy kill jobs were so much simpler.

As Daniel finishes kicking away the body of the rat before him, he frowns. Something was wrong. It takes him only a moment more before he realizes what the issue is — light. Light that glowed blue and that shimmered slightly as it reflected off the dark water that ran through the center of the sewer was coming around the corner. Now that he is paying attention, Daniel also realizes that there's a creaking of a cart moving along slowly as well.

Asin hisses slightly and pulls out her daggers, tucking the rat tail away as she steps up next to Daniel. Cat eyes gleam in the dark, reflecting light as she slowly moves forward, followed quickly by Daniel.

The hooded figures turn the corner, a single tall figure leading the way as a cart is pushed along behind him. The figure holds a hand up as he spots Asin and Daniel, lips pulling apart and showing a series of sharp, needle teeth. The Beastkin lets out a low growl, a hand falling to the knife at his side.

Before Daniel can reach for his shield, Asin lets out a low hiss and growl, replying to the Beastkin in the common tongue of their kind. The Beastkin hesitates and then moves forward slowly though Daniel does not fail to notice that his companions have retrieved a pair of crossbows.

A yowly, growly conversation ensues between the stranger and Asin for a few minutes. Finally, out of patience, Daniel elbows his companion gently and asks. "What is going on?"

"Smugglers," Asin replies and gestures to the group.

"Oh…" Daniel tightens his grip on his mace, an act that has the Beastkin tense and Asin shaking her head.

"No, leave. Not our business," Asin insists.

"I…" Daniel frowns, considering. Asin is technically correct – they are not the Guards. However, letting them smuggle some unknown substance or person in did not sit well with Daniel either. "What are they smuggling?"

"Sabu," the answer is a low, rumbly growl that sets the hair on the back of Daniel's neck tingling.

"Oh." The alcoholic drink that was prized by the Beastkin was certainly tasty, but it seemed a bit excessive to smuggle.

"Tax. Very high," Asin answers the unasked question. She frowns, growling back to the Beastkin who answers in Brad.

"Five times the cost of Sabu," the Beastkin growls, spitting to the side at the end.

Daniel's eyes widen, mind going back to the size of the population and how many there's are of them. For a moment more, he considers before he slowly slides his mace back into its loop. The Beastkin sees the gestures of peace and gestures for his men to continue pulling the cart, stopping as they pass by to throw over a wineskin that Asin deftly catches.

A quick sniff is all that is needed to confirm the contents before Asin stores the skin. Daniel eyes the skin for a moment, wondering if it is a bribe or a gesture of gratitude. In the end, did it really matter? He had made his decision. "Come on; we've got rats to kill."

Chapter 12

"Sure?" Asin prods Daniel again as the young Adventurers fights to contain his yawns. Up early in the morning to meet the caravan to Karlak, the pair are walking through the city with their gear on their back. The two and a half weeks in Silverstone had passed in a blur of quests, and now, it was time to head home.

"Yes." Daniel nods firmly. As tempting as the offer to join a guild was, he could not choose it now. Would not, perhaps. He had a quest that needed completing, a Dungeon that he had never seen the end of and a girlfriend he had to confess too. In truth, a part of Daniel knows he is putting the decision off, procrastinating.

Asin continues to chew on the improvised bread wrap she has made, content to let Daniel make the choice without interference. She understood she was not truly wanted by the guild - they would not decline her if she joined with Daniel but she was not their target. If Daniel went, she would follow - the more advanced the dungeon, the more coin there was after all. If he did not, she would get there eventually. In either case, Asin knows her pig-headed partner would not abandon her.

As they come up to the caravan, Asin prods Daniel to take over the conversation, content to let him do the talking. Being in a new city, she had done more talking than she was used to. While she would never tell Daniel, her throat was raw from squeezing out words in Brad. It was so much easier to speak in Catkin and perhaps partly why she had gotten involved with Tevfik so fast. Her tail lashed again as she thought of the Catkin and his luxurious fur, the way he used to nibble on her ear…

Daniel quietly moves slightly further away from his growling friend, having gotten used to the occasional switches in her temperament in the last few weeks. Tevfik had hurt her, more than she was willing to let on and once again, Daniel wonders how old his friend really was. Was Tevfik perhaps her first real relationship?

Pushing aside those thoughts, Daniel focuses on the job at hand and greets the caravan master, getting their orders. It would be a long few weeks back to Karlak.

***

Later that day, when things have settled, and the caravan is on its way, Daniel finally pulls up the information on his Status. It was time to allocate his attribute and skill points. He had avoided the topic for days, not feeling the need to rush as the simple low-level Quests that were offered to them were easily dealt with by their existing skills.

Now, with nothing more to do but watch the surroundings and his decision to turn down the guild offers, he could focus on leveling up.

First, it was time to adjust his skills. Of course, he could upgrade his existing skills making each better and more effective, but Daniel was more curious about the new skills he had the option to learn.

Now that he had upgraded his Healing skills and knew the human body better, he had access to two different spells - **Cure Serious Wounds** or **Healer's Mark**. The first was a more powerful version of his current spell, providing almost instantaneous healing but at a higher mana cost. Healer's Mark however just accelerated the healing process of the target over a period of time, allowing the target's body to do the majority of the healing. It was significantly more mana efficient than either of the instantaneous spells and was very popular among Healers who needed to conserve their mana. It did have the potential of failure though - if the host body was not strong enough, the spell would fail to heal the wounds fully and would instead use a significant portion of the target's resources, causing the death of the target.

In terms of his offensive skills, he could now learn **Shield Rush** which was a progression on the **Shield Bash** skill he already knew. Instead of a static attack, Shield Rush would allow him to attack using his shield at a distance by charging the monsters, allowing him to layer a stun and knockback attack. While not as versatile as Shield Bash, Shield Rush was extremely powerful against single opponents, and the Stun effects normally lasted longer too.

His archery skills were still not sufficient to give him any Skill options, but he did have several Club options to review. **Power Strike** continued to be available while two additional options had opened up - **Crushing Blow** and **Perin's Blow**. Crushing Blow was a variation on Power Strike which did less overall damage but which gave additional bonuses against medium to heavily armored opponents. The skill focused on destroying and smashing through armor with pure strength and at higher levels was known for ignoring even physical damage resistances. Perin's Wrath, on the other hand, provided a knockback effect that if used correctly could even throw a monster into the air for follow-on attacks. A similar skill had been what Niko had used to finish off the Overseer in the dungeon.

In addition to all these, Daniel had also gained a few additional passive skill options including **Sprint**, **Greater Endurance** and exclusive to him, **Martyr's Strength**. The last made Daniel pull up the detailed information again to review.

Martyr's Strength

A unique skill brought about by the ongoing usage of Martyr's Touch on the individual's body. Combines an innate understanding of the owner's body with the user's unique Gift to increase regeneration rates.
Skill: Passive
Cost: N/A
Effect: User has a permanent increase of 10% to Health and Stamina regeneration.

In the end, Daniel closes the screen again and rubs at his chin. There were so many options to choose from that Daniel sits quietly, attempting to structure his thoughts. If he focused on his most likely opponents in the near future - the Ogres - both Crushing Blow and Shield Rush would benefit him the most. However, the use of Perin's Blow with his other skills could allow Daniel to inflict significant damage on a single target in a short period of time. In fact, over time, Perin's Blow probably could become the linchpin of his attacks against a tough opponent.

However, that would not benefit him in a fight against smaller opponents. If he upgraded his Double Strike ability, he'd be able to attack four times in quick order, making him a much deadlier opponent against multiple individuals. It would have made him significantly stronger against the Imps for starters.

Healer's Mark would always be useful especially over the course of a day. It would ensure they could stay in tip-top condition while they fought and when they increased their party, it would be even more important as Daniel's mana pool was highly limited.

If he wanted to be selfish, he could even take his unique Skill and increase his health and stamina regeneration. The significant increase in both would make it easier for him in dungeon levels and everyday life though it was probably the least useful group skill.

It was not a simple choice and one that Daniel had agonized over for hours now. Worst, he knew that these kinds of decisions would come even more often as he developed in strength.

***

Later that evening Asin prods Daniel, taking him out of his contemplation as he prods at the fire. "Skills?"

Daniel pauses, staring at the fire before he finally answers her, "I chose to get Perin's Blow."

Perin's Blow

Named after the God of Storms, Perin, this strike sends concentrates the force of the user's blow to create a knockback effect against its target.

Skill: Active

Cost: 25 Stamina

Effect: User's Strike does 15% more damage and knocks back target. Knockback level dependent on user's strength, Club skill, weight and size of the target and striking area.

"It's a knockback effect, kind of like Niko's," Daniel explains, before continuing, "I think it'd be useful against the Crawlers and Ogres, and if I learn to use it right, it should also allow me to control where the monsters move during a fight."

Asin just nods as Daniel calls up his Status Screen once more, hoping he made the right choice. When he got back, he would ask Khy'ra to teach him Healer's Mark. It was a spell that he had watched her cast before, one of the few Healer spells that the Elf knew. If she was still willing to speak with him after he told her what he had done.

| Name: Daniel Chai |
| Class: Level 6 Adventurer (14%) |

Sub-classes: Level 7 (Miner) (14%)
Human (Male)

Statistics
Life: 229
Stamina: 229
Mana: 168

Attributes
Strength: 22
Agility: 20
Constitution: 28
Intelligence: 17
Willpower: 18
Luck: 13

Skills
Unarmed Combat: Level 3 (37/100)
Clubs: Level 9 (04/100)
Archery: Level 2 (18/100_
Shield: Level 7 (84/100)
Dodge: Level 5 (12/100)
Combat Sense: Level 5 (98/100)
Perception: Level 6 (07/100)
Mining: Level 7 (78/100)
Healing: Level 8 (89/100)
Herb Lore: Level 3 (31/100)
Stealth: Level 2 (14/100)
Cooking: Level 3 (21/100)
Singing: Level 2 (14/100)

Skill Proficiencies

Double Strike
Shield Bash
Perin's Blow
Mapping (II)

Spells
Minor Healing (I)

Gifts
Martyr's Touch - The caster may heal oneself or others by touch and concentration, sacrificing a portion of his life to do so. Cost varies depending on the extent of the injuries healed.

Pushing aside those thoughts, Daniel stands and moves to the back of the caravan. He had made his decision. Better to keep busy and that meant helping others. Interestingly enough, the hanger-ons from Silverstone seemed both less numerous and better fed than before, so Daniel expects that he will have less to do.

***

Days pass in quiet contemplation and evening bouts of training. The other Adventuring group that hired on with this caravan were highly insular, refusing to interact with Daniel and Asin outside of the bare minimum. After overhearing a particular conversation about the Catkin, Daniel was more than happy to keep it that way. As always, Asin just shrugs and moves on with her life, not letting the slight affect her.

Without other Adventurers to train with, Daniel finds himself working with the caravan guards. Once word of his free healing made the rounds, even the caravan manager had taken to speaking with Daniel in more friendly terms - if nothing more than to soothe his ulcerous stomach. The caravan guards were more than happy to train with Daniel for his aid, whether it was for magical or non-magical healing.

A week and a half after they leave Silverstone, the caravan meets its first sign of trouble. The other Adventurers having left to complete another quest, the caravan is sparsely guarded for its size. The lack of guards has resulted in Daniel and Asin having to stand guard every evening, cutting into precious sleeping time. As Daniel rolls over to grab his mace after being woken to take his turn, an arrow strikes his bedroll. For a moment, Daniel just squats there, staring at the arrow as he attempts to understand this strange feathered disturbance.

"Attack!" roars one of the guards and the shout makes Daniel move, automatically reaching for his shield. Crouching low with his shield in front of him, he searches for the attackers and spots a good dozen bearing down on him. Another scream from behind makes Daniel turn, and he spots another dozen human bandits, making Daniel's mouth run dry. They are out outnumbered two to one, and many of the guards are still struggling awake.

Making a snap decision, Daniel rushes the group ahead of him, holding his shield in front of his body. While he might not have the skill, there was no reason he could not use his shield as a battering ram, and so he does, ducking low and scooping his arm as he runs into his opponent. For once, his shorter than normal stature benefits Daniel and the screaming, dirty bandit is flipped over his shoulder to smash into the ground. His first opponent taken care of, Daniel's grin widens, and he stands swiftly, engaging his Double Strike to crush the arm and then knee of his next opponent, flashes of electricity lighting up their fight. As the downed bandit begins to roll over, Asin pounces onto him and shoves a blade into his throat. With the blade caught, she leaves it in his throat as she draws a throwing knife to provide Daniel further support, hissing in anger at the blood that coats her pants.

His second opponent crippled, Daniel spins and steps forward quickly to his next adversary, engaging Perin's Blow for the first time in combat. Daniel strikes low, and to the side, the bandit's clumsy block is smashed aside as the mace catches him on the hip and sends him bowling into the line behind him. Grinning in elation at the successful use of his Skill, Daniel wipes the spray of spittle off his face as Asin works her knives and a bolo into the struggling pile, tangling the group before casting an enchanted oil flask into the mass.

Daniel can feel the heat behind his back, drying his shirt as he steps forward to deal with another bandit, ignoring the screams of pain and the smell of charred meat. He catches the first strike high and raises his mace to strike high but an arrow slams into his unarmored torso, spinning him around. Daniel screams, the coarse wood of the arrow shaft digging into his muscles as he stumbles away from his attacker, a second arrow missing by inches.

Daniel's attacker follows up, swinging his sword once and then again, both blows caught by Daniel's shield as the Adventurer hides behind it. Stepping forward, his attacker hooks his foot behind Daniel's and pulls, dropping the Adventurer onto his back and eliciting an involuntary scream as the arrow in his chest shifts. As Daniel recovers from the fall, the bandit thrusts and Daniel feels the blade sliding into him and grating along his ribs.

Asin meanwhile has spun away from her finished opponent but is forced to dodge to the side as the archer fires, again and again, ensuring that the Catkin is unable to close the distance to her partner. She snarls, her thrown weapons unable to reach the cowardly archer. Not given a choice, Asin jumps back again as the archer fires and throws a knife, activating her newest Skill Fan of Knives. Her single knife transforms into four, each newly created knife mirroring the original's flight path and plunging into Daniel's attacker's back and forcing the bandit away. Even as she lands, Asin rolls and comes up, catching and sliding a short sword that thrusts at her in an attempt to catch the Catkin unaware. She snarls, the blade scoring her shoulder as she fails to entirely divert the attack, jade eyes turning back to her downed partner in worry.

Given a moment's respite, Daniel grabs and pulls the arrow out and then casts a Minor Healing on himself, whimpering in pain as his body forcefully heals the wound closed. The puncture in his chest closes slightly as well, sufficiently enough that Daniel can focus and pull the shield across his body. It is not a moment too soon as an arrow smashes into the shield as the archer attempts to kill the downed Adventurer. Still injured, Daniel is forced to cast another Minor Healing before he is able to stagger to his feet.

Lips pulled tight, Daniel totters to the side, both fighters swaying slightly from their injuries. As his opponent closes on him again, Daniel focuses and triggers a Shield Bash, slamming the shield forward into his opponent's face before he finishes the fight by braining his opponent with his mace.

Realizing that Asin is hard-pressed by two attackers, he rushes over to aid her, barely dodging another arrow. The momentary distraction of the short, stout adventurer is enough for Asin to spin away and draw a throwing knife, sending a Piercing Throw deep into the groin of an attacker and dropping him.

A sudden scream abruptly cuts-off from where the archer shoots at the pair, his demise swiftly ended by a second bolt. Waggoneers, woken from their sleep grab at crossbows and clubs to aid the guards and the Adventurers finally. For a moment the last of the bandits' pause, wavering as they realize so many of their comrades have fallen.

Daniel does not pause, throwing another brutal blow into his opponent's stomach with Perin's Blow, throwing the bandit up into the air. Still, Daniel does not pause even though he struggles to breathe, triggering a Double Strike as the man is in the air, slamming blows into the body and casting blood into the air.

The brutal attack is the last straw for the untrained, ill-equipped group. Screaming, the bandits flee back into the forest, letting Daniel collapse onto the ground in exhaustion. All his strength used up; he begins to feel the injuries that cover his body. When Daniel is finally able to focus, he taps into his Gift to finally finish closing the wounds in his chest. Memories shift, fading away, but for once, Daniel ignores the cost for the pure pleasure of being free of pain. When the wounds are finally closed, Daniel pushes himself up, ignoring the numerous smaller wounds across his body. He has others to heal.

As always, the aftermath of a battle is a sad affair. The smell of iron and voided bowels fills the camp, along with the stifled cries of pain and the slow dragging of bodies as the caravan guards first finish off the seriously wounded and then dispose of the bandits' bodies. No one objected - bandits were the lowest of the low and were killed on sight in Brad, and the caravan had lost many. Three waggoneers had been slain in their sleep, another two guards dead before Daniel can make his way to them. Numerous others carry injuries, too insignificant for Daniel to waste mana or his Gift on.

When the healing he can do is done, the caravan master comes over and offers Daniel a drink. Daniel gratefully takes it, coughing slightly as the spirit burns its way down his throat.

"Bad luck this trip," the caravan master said.

Daniel can only nod, waving Asin over. She sniffs, taking the bottle while Daniel lets a finger linger on her palm, sending his Gift into her body to check for injuries. Finding nothing more than a few treated cuts and a pulled lower back muscle, he leaves her alone.

"Thank you," the caravan master adds, stroking his mustache absently. "It would have been worse without you two."

Asin can only nod again, too tired to suggest a monetary bonus. Perhaps later if the caravan master did not make the offer himself. For now, there were still bodies to put aside and fires to rekindle and a watch to be set.

***

It is only later that night when others are asleep that Daniel finds a moment of peace. Having offered the excuse that he needed to wait for his mana to regenerate, Daniel hunkers in a corner away from the gathered bodies; his trembling hands clutched beneath his cloak. Daniel forces himself to breathe through his mouth, the smell of blood reminding him of what just transpired.

So close. He had been so close to dying. If his opponent had shifted his aim a few inches, he would have pierced his heart. If the archer had fired an inch lower, the arrow would have pierced his liver, probably incapacitating him for the rest of the fight and ensuring his death.

Daniel at first tries to stop the shaking but eventually gives in, letting his body shudder and tremble as it reacts to his near-death. His mind replays the incident over and over again, and for a bitter moment, Daniel wishes his Gift would have taken those memories. Damn thing – it took memories of evenings with Khy'ra and evening conversations with his Grandfather but left memories like this and being turned by Pearl.

Slowly, his body stops trembling, his mind becoming less of a jumbled mess. Looking up, Daniel sees a streak of blood, and he wonders if it was a bandits' or a friend's. Damn them. Orcs, monsters, Dungeons and more existed, and yet, these bandits felt the need to attack other sentients. There were so many ways to make a living with Skills, but somehow, these scum felt the need to attack others for their living. Lips curling up in disgust, Daniel growls softly. Damn them.

***

Days later, the caravan has pulled to a stop near a river bend, sheltered from the rain by a copse of trees and from attack on two sides by the river. The group is more relaxed now, the caravan master having found replacements for the guards at the next town they had stopped in along with another Adventuring group. That evening, after dinner, Daniel walks to the water to fill his waterskin and finds Asin sitting by herself.

"Asin?"

At her name being called, the Catkin scrubs at her face before she looks to Daniel. Black fur is plastered down by tears, dark green eyes daring Daniel to mention her weakness. He knows better, instead choosing to sit down next to his partner in silent companionship.

As the silence stretches to the breaking point, Asin finally speaks. "Tevfik liked me. Yes?"

"Yes, I think so," Daniel replies and she nods jerkily.

"Stupid," she mutters, claws coming out to knead her knees. She stares at them for a time, disgusted at her own actions, for reacting so emotionally and blaming him. Yet, she had truly felt betrayed. "I liked him."

"I know."

"No future," Asin says again, rubbing at her knees. "Stupid."

"To fall in love?"

"No love. Like," Asin insists, glaring at Daniel who offers a quick nod. "Stupid anyway."

"Why?" Daniel frowns, on uncertain ground now. After all, they were consenting adults.

"Because over. Always. I leave. He leave. Stupid," Asin insists, shaking her head. "You, Khy'ra, stupid."

"Hey!" Daniel glares at his friend, waving a finger at her. "Just because you don't agree doesn't mean it's stupid. Khy'ra and I are adults. We know what we're doing."

"Stupid. Get hurt," Asin states again.

"Maybe. No, certainly. But in-between, I know a smart, wise, tough, and beautiful Elf," Daniel points out, shaking his head. "We know what's coming, but that doesn't mean we can't enjoy it."

"Still stupid."

"Yes, but it's a good kind of stupid."

Asin lets out a chuff of frustration and then puts her head on her knees again, her tail uncurling from her back slowly. "Hurts."

"Yes," Daniel sighs, unsure of what else to say. So, he says nothing.

After a time, Asin stands up, moving back to the fire. As she passes, she pauses to say, "Thank you."

When she is gone, Daniel stares back into the water, thinking of Khy'ra and the talk he must have. Stupid. Yeah, it probably was.

Chapter 13

"Daniel!" Khy'ra gasps, smiling up at the adventurer as he steps into her Clinic. Weeks of travel with the caravan had finally taken them back to Karlak without further incident of note. This time around, the trip had passed through numerous villages and a few towns but none with Beginner Dungeons. The pair had spent their time at these new settlements sightseeing, for the most part, each stop no longer than a day and often only a few hours. Slightly spooked, the wagons had moved at a quicker pace than normal, and so the pair had arrived in Karlak a day early. Having delivered their goods to an enthused Maxwell, the pair had split up immediately.

Daniel smiles, stepping forwards and wrapping his arms around Khy'ra, kissing her passionately before pulling away as sudden guilt flashes through him. Seeing the change in expression, Khy'ra stops and pushes at him gently, murmuring, "What's wrong?"

"I…" Daniel frowns, searching for a way to say this before just going with the bald truth. "I slept with someone else."

"Oh…" Khy'ra sighs and steps back, blue eyes raking over the man. They glimmer for a moment as she does so before she speaks. "Was she pretty?"

"Umm… a bit," Daniel says.

"A bit," Khy'ra repeats and Daniel nods. "Really? Just a bit?"

"I was drunk!" Daniel adds, grimacing. "I'm sorry, it's not an excuse."

"It's not, but I'm not angry about you sleeping with her," Khy'ra says and smiles slightly at Daniel. "We never made any promises to each other after all. And really, I've been alive and will be alive for many more years. I'll have many more lovers than you, dear boy, so why would I begrudge you yours?"

Daniel blinks, then nods slightly, exhaling. His reasoning had been along those lines too but… his thoughts fall to disarray as Khy'ra raises a finger.

"But, I am disappointed about the betrayal," Khy'ra continues, blue eyes flashing again.

"You just said…" Daniel stutters, confused.

"Not me, yourself." She taps with her finger at his chest, continuing, "You felt it was wrong, did you not? So, it matters not whether I viewed it wrong, you betrayed yourself. And for that, I am disappointed."

Daniel opens his mouth and then shuts it, blinking in understanding. She was right - he had struggled with his actions. He had chosen poorly, and he had felt guilty about it - and even if she did not think it was a betrayal, it was one of himself.

"Oh…"

"For that, dear boy, I must enact suitable punishment," Khy'ra continues, stepping forward and then pushing gently at Daniel, guiding him out of the door. Daniel opens his mouth then shuts it under the firm gaze of the blonde Elf. The door shut on him, Daniel grimaces and stares at the empty Clinic, wondering what to do. After all, he had sent everyone home.

Inside the room, Khy'ra leans against the door, eyes half-closed. She bit her lips, turning to look at the door, a hand raised briefly before dropping it and turning to her desk and the paperwork that awaited her.

***

"Late!" Asin grumbles at Daniel as he hurries up to her at the Dungeon entrance. He flashes her an apologetic shrug of his shoulders having spent the night drinking alone. His head pounded, and he still wasn't sure - were they broken up permanently? Or just that night? Should he try to see her again tonight? His rambling thoughts are brought to a stop as Asin asks. "Ready?"

"Yes." Daniel shakes his head and winces, finally giving in and casting a Minor Healing on himself to clear the hangover. It was not a good idea to go into a Dungeon, even one as familiar as Karlak, distracted and in pain. He forcibly pushes thoughts of Khy'ra aside and does a final check of his weaponry and armor, adjusting his backpack before they finally enter the Dungeon for the seventh floor.

"Mine?" Daniel asks as they spot their first Ogre. Asin just yawns, hiding her teeth with her furry hand. Not waiting any further, Daniel rushes the Ogre that has started running to him, focusing on the battle.

He staggers his steps, breaking his timing for a brief moment to throw off the Ogre's swing, letting the club pass by him before he steps in and engages Perin's Blow. The blow from under the monster with his mace pushes the mace into the creature's body, throwing the creature upwards long enough for Daniel to slam the rim of his shield into its airborne body. The Ogre falls back, doubled over by repeated strikes to its stomach and diaphragm, and Daniel takes the time to line up an overhand strike on its head. He bends with his knees, putting his weight behind each attack before repeating the strike again and again, never letting up, even as the Ogre attempts to hit him as well.

As Daniel stands over the dispersing body, breathing heavily, Asin calls out a warning and points. In the distance, a trio of Ogres is jogging to the pair to take revenge. Sliding his mace into his belt again, he reaches for his crossbow and loads a bolt quickly, sighting down the weapon before firing. Hours of practice has made loading the crossbow much smoother, Daniel's considerable strength aiding in this endeavor. The bolt flies through the sky, slamming into a thigh and Daniel curses as he works the crossbow. He was aiming for the Ogre to the right of this one. Could he not do anything right?

Asin steps up to buy Daniel time, throwing a pair of blades that blossom into a storm as she activates her Skill. The Ogres duck and twist, attempting to dodge the thrown weapons. Most of the knives miss except for a pair that embed in the unlucky, injured Ogre. The creature groans, blades and arrow embedded in its body and noticeably slows down its movement. Loaded, Daniel aims and fires another bolt, this one targeted to finish off the injured Ogre, and with the close range, he manages to hit.

The remaining pair of Ogres finally reach the two Adventurers, forcing Daniel to drop the crossbow to his side and pull out his mace. A slight smile crossing his face at their ability to injure one of the opponents significantly, Daniel steps forward to the monster on the right while Asin fades to the left, tossing her knives with more care.

Her opponent swings its club at her, forcing the young Catkin to dart forward and to the side, raking the exposed arm with her blade, her enchanted aura sending electricity through the contact and forcing the arm to spasm.

Daniel's Ogre stops just outside of its range, swinging first one then the other arm as it wields two crude, short clubs. Unable to find a good opportunity, Daniel feints to the left and then ducks right, aiming for the last injured opponent that is struggling back to its feet. He feels a club glance off his shield, the blow sending tremors through his body as the Ogre instinctively lashes out and then he's pass and rushing the last Ogre.

He triggers his Double Strike skill the moment he gets into range, taking his new opponent's attack on his shield with a grunt and feeling his arm and shoulder compress, flaring in pain under the heavy strike. Still, he stays focused and lands both blows, sending electricity dancing through the monster at the points of impact, darting to the right immediately as the monster exhales, washing him with its fetid breath. The Ogre finds it difficult to keep up with his smaller and faster opponent, injured as it is and for a moment, Daniel finds himself facing its back. Twisting at his hips, Daniel puts as much strength into the next attack that he can while triggering Perin's Blow, smashing his mace into the Ogre's back, targeting its kidney and sending it flying into its brethren.

The Ogre lets out a breathless scream, bowling over the other monster before expiring and breaking apart. As the other Ogre attempts to stand, pushing upwards with one hand supporting it, Daniel closes in. The stout Adventurer targets its free arm, raining blows on the fragile forearm bones and shattering them to make the monster release its weapon. Devoid of its second club, Daniel alternates strikes with the monster, no longer forced back by the attacks.

Asin, meanwhile, weaves under each attack thrown at her, slashing and stabbing at the exposed arm till the Ogre's arm finally loses all strength and its club drops. She then proceeds to cut and stab the monster, ducking under increasingly desperate attacks, always dodging by the smallest margins, relying on speed and skill. Each attack sends light dancing, making the creature flinch again and again. As her opponent finally collapses, she turns to Daniel to find him beating on his opponent.

Unfortunately, a night spent drinking and thoughts about Khy'ra make him slow and sloppy. An overhand blow that should be easy enough to block comes crashing down onto Daniel's shield. The block is just a touch too slow, the angle wrong and instead of being caught fully, the club smashes past the shield and skips off, glancing off to land a blow on Daniel's temple. He staggers, and before he can recover, a backhanded strike connects with his temple, knocking Daniel out.

Asin yelps, throwing a Piercing Shot before the Ogre can land a third blow. The knife drills into the Ogre's arm, forcing it to drop its weapon even as she charges forward to protect her friend.

***

When Daniel awakens, he does so with the taste of a dead rat in his mouth. He coughs, pain shooting through his head as his tender temple rings. He whimpers, curling up slightly as pain washes over him, his vision shimmering in and out of focus. Staying silent, he concentrates on his Gift, pulling it from his core to search for the cause of his pain.

Bruising on his face, a cracked skull and minor swelling in his brain from an incipient concussion were the main culprits. Better, much better than he had expected truth be told. Focusing, he lowers the swelling and stitches the skull back together with his Gift to give him relief from the pain before he begins to cast his Minor Healing spell to finish the job.

As Daniel finally opens his eyes fully, he sees Asin squatting a short distance away watching over him. He shudders, remembering the sickening crack of wood on bone, the flash of pain and then, nothing.

"You saved me," Daniel says, working his mouth. "You used a healing potion, too, didn't you?"

Asin nods and then shrugs. Of course she did, they were partners. That was what they did after all.

"Thanks," Daniel says and stands, his body mostly healed. Fighting distracted on this level was a bad idea. Without a full set of heavier armor, any lucky blow could cause problems. Of course, getting a helmet would probably be a good idea, but Daniel was leery of spending the coin for it when he was going to get a full set of better armor soon.

"Ready?" Asin growls and Daniel pauses, rubbing at the dried blood on his temple.

"No... not really," Daniel decides suddenly, shaking his head. "I'm sorry, perhaps we can try this on another day?"

Asin nods. She was not sure what it was, but Daniel was obviously not all here today. Grimacing, she turns to pick her way back to the dungeon entrance. Ah well, she'll head back up to the fifth floor by herself then. No reason to not earn more coin even if her partner was taking the day off.

***

"Daniel!" Litzburn, the Master-of-Arms at the training grounds calls out in greeting, walking over to the young Adventurer as he enters. The large, ebony-skinned master-at-arms smiles at his former student, shaking Daniel's hand with his own scarred, calloused one. "Are you here to train?"

"Yes, I think so," Daniel says.

"That's not a very sure answer." Litzburn chuckles, running a hand over his bald scalp to clear some sweat. "What's wrong?"

"Nothing. Just, a lot on my mind." Daniel shakes his head, glancing at the training weapons. "Maybe I'll just work the bags for a bit."

"You're always welcome here," Litzburn says, waving goodbye to Daniel as he returns to his other students.

Later, after Daniel has settled in, and Litzburn has watched the young man work the training posts desolutely, he walks over and taps Daniel on his shoulder. So lost in thought is the young Adventurer that he completely misses Litzburn's approach. "Enough. You're shaming me and yourself. You won't learn anything but bad habits doing that."

Daniel's lips twist, and he hangs his head, rubbing the back of his neck as he apologizes, "Sorry."

"Come. Let's talk." Waving to his sub-instructors to take over, he walks the young Adventurer to a nearby bench. The older man has quickly figured out the potential cause of the issue. "Problems with Khy'ra?"

"Yes. No. Maybe," Daniel answers immediately and then stops, collecting his thoughts properly. "It's not just that. It's… well, can I ask some advice?"

"Certainly."

Speaking hurriedly, Daniel blurts out the entire story of the guilds, of being asked, again and again, to join, of the potential benefits offered. He speaks fast, trying to get the story out and along the way, he mentions his issues with Khy'ra too, of how he cheated - but it wasn't really cheating, except it was - and what happened. In the end, he runs down while Litzburn just nods. It is a good thing that Daniel speaks with his head down, for at times, Litzburn's lips twitch and amusement dances in the older man's eyes. Ah, the tragedies of youth.

"I would not despair, I do not think that the Elf will cast you aside for such a matter. I believe your current predicament is punishment enough," Litzburn says, lips twitching again before he continues. "I believe you will not make the same mistake again, no?"

"Yes. Ummm… No? I won't make that mistake again." Daniel nods firmly. "It was stupid. And… Not that good."

"Mmm… You bed an Elf, young one. And one who I understand is still quite energetic between the sheets. I fear if you compare your future companions to her, you will be inevitably disappointed," Litzburn replies and then claps him on the back. "At least technically. There is much to be said for passion though."

"Oh. Right." Realizing what he is speaking about, Daniel flushes and looks down, suddenly uncomfortable. "Right."

"As for your problem with the guilds, few in this hall would find your circumstance a problem. Guilds rarely chase after melee fighters," Litzburn waves his hand around the training hall where his students work hard to hone their abilities. "Still, that is little comfort for you. For myself, I joined the moment I could - though that was after I completed my own Beginner Dungeon. Mary, on the other hand, waited for many years before she did, preferring to adventure on her own."

"Mary has a guild?" Daniel perks up, remembering his earliest friend and the owner of the school he sits in.

"Yes, but hers would not fit you. She joined the White Scales, and they only recruit Expert Adventurers and up," Litzburn answers. "If you decide to join a guild, be sure to understand what they ask for and what is required to leave them. Each guild must register their charter and members with the Adventurer's Guild itself, so it's always best to speak with them directly."

"Thank you," Daniel nods, standing up finally. Well, at least he had learned a little more, but mentioning the Guild reminded Daniel that there was another who he could ask for advice. "I think I'm done for the day."

"Yes, I certainly agree," Litzburn chuckles, clapping the younger Adventurer on the back. "Come back another day. We still need to work on your form."

***

"Afternoon, Liev." After standing in line, Daniel is finally able to speak with the scruffy, red-headed attendant.

The middle-aged man looks up, rubbing at an ink splotch on his fingers absently. "Daniel. I see you are back. Did you just return?"

"No, we arrived last night. I was hoping to speak with you?" Daniel gestures over to the tables to the side and Liev nods, waving one of the other attendants to take over his spot.

"What is this about?' Liev sits, noting the absence of Asin and wondering if there are issues with the pairing. It was after all not uncommon for adventuring parties to break up.

Once again, Daniel speaks of his invitations to join the guilds, leaving out his issues with Khy'ra. He was still somewhat embarrassed he discussed the matter with Litzburn and was certainly not going to bring it up again, especially with Liev. After he is done, Liev sits silently, staring at the younger man and then sighs, fingers rubbing together again as he scrubs at the ink spot. "I'm sorry, Daniel. I should have informed you about them before you left."

"It's fine," Daniel says immediately.

"No, I should have warned you. I knew local groups would want to work with you, but I had forgotten your generosity with your healing gifts. It was bound to attract attention on your travels,"

Liev continues before shaking his head. "I should have warned you."

"Warned me?" Eyebrows lowering, Daniel squints at Liev as he considers the words.

"Yes. The guilds that Adventurers make within ours, they are both a great help and a great hindrance," Liev says. "We have had to forcefully disband more than one group, relieving the leaders of their membership and reassigning Adventurers. It is a lot of work because some can't handle the power that such a group can provide. The benefits they speak of are true, but many groups also attempt to control their members quite firmly for these benefits.

"I would have wanted you to avoid their attention for a while longer, but it is done. For now, I recommend you complete your current quest. Whatever your decision, being both more experienced and with better armor will stand you in better favor."

"Should I join one then? Litzburn suggested I do."

"Litzburn did well with his guild before he retired. Others haven't been as lucky," Liev answers immediately. "If I were you, I would not trust my ability to others, no matter how kind they seem."

A wry grin twists his face as Daniel nods. Right. His Gift. He had forgotten again how that could make things more difficult for him. "Thanks, Liev."

"It is a big decision, Daniel. Take your time making it," Liev says, smiling and stands. "Now, if that is all…?"

Daniel nods absently, letting the man leave as he falls back into thought. Neither of these men had helped him make a decision. Well, except perhaps about Khy'ra.

***

"Daniel," Khy'ra smiles slightly, having spoken only after watching as Daniel finishes wrapping up the cut on the carpenter's arm. The carpenter bobs a head in thanks to both, heading out of the examination room to drop a coin in the donation jar.

"Khy'ra," Daniel answers, shifting slightly. Having nothing more to do and tired of thinking, he had come to the Clinic to work.

"How are you?"

"I'm… well." Daniel rubs at his neck, extending a hand tentatively. Khy'ra crosses over, taking it and he smiles slightly, relaxing.

"I'm… sorry," said Daniel.

"As I said, you have nothing to be sorry to me about. Your apology should be to yourself," she says, leaning forwards and kissing him gently. "I just wanted you to think it over."

Daniel nods, "Yeah. I think I understand what you were saying."

"Good," she smiles slightly, giving him a hug. "I just wanted to say hi. There's still a lot of work to do. But we can speak, tonight?"

"Tonight," Daniel replies, smiling and returning the hug before reluctantly letting her go.

***

"So, you've been approached by the guilds then. At least, they don't know of your Gift," Khy'ra says, looking up at him from his chest as they lie on her bed.

"Yeah, Liev says it would be worst if they did," Daniel answers. "It's stupid really; it's not as if I could use it during combat or something."

"Mmm…. You are too used to having it, Daniel. Having your party, your entire guild constantly in top shape? Not having to spend gold on potions? It would be a great help. Too many groups find themselves forced to either work partly injured or tired or spending large sums on potions. And on longer delves in more advanced dungeons? Your Gift would be a lifesaver," Khy'ra says. "You have a lot of power here, a lot of leeways."

Daniel slowly nods, absently letting his hand run down her bare back, feeling the smooth skin under his fingers, "So you think I should join a guild?"

"Mmm… I think you shouldn't stop doing that. And that you should remember your earlier lesson."

Daniel pauses, hand hovering for a moment. Earlier lesson? Oh… As he begins to put it together, he finds his thoughts interrupted by soft lips. Right - some other things take precedence.

Chapter 14

"Morning, Asin." Daniel greets his friend, up bright and early and waiting at the Dungeon entrance. She nods in greeting, sniffs once and smiles slightly. Daniel sighs, realizing that his surprise had been given away by her superior senses. He reaches into his backpack, extracting the sandwich for the Catkin who devours the stacked bacon and ham delicacy.

When she is finished, Daniel says, "I think we should focus on the seventh floor for now. Farm it for as much stone as we can. If we ask Liev for the conversion rate for the two B Grade stones for the smaller stones, we can focus on just getting the smaller stones. I think it'll be safer for us rather than risking, well, deeper levels. What do you think?"

Asin nods in agreement. Yesterday's experience a stark reminder that while skill and tactics made a difference, they were both under-equipped and under-leveled. One small mistake could end in tragedy.

Resolved, the pair head down once more to the seventh floor, intent on just farming the Ogres for their stones. No risky attacks, no pushing things. Slow and steady was what they would do.

***

"Yahooo!" Screaming, the half-naked Adventurer runs ahead of the pair, throwing himself at a pair of Ogres the two had earlier targeted. Running behind him, his friends call out a quick apology as they overtake the two to back up their friend.

"Hey!" Daniel grumbles, lowering his crossbow. Damn it. That was the second time that day that this group had stolen one of their kills.

Asin chuffs out too in anger, her tail lashing sideways as she watches as the five adventurers split the Ogres. The half-naked warrior with the oversized sword takes on a single Ogre by himself while his friends work on the last, crippling and killing it quickly. They work smoothly together, constantly harrying and attacking the Ogre in such a way that the monster is never able to fully focus on any one member.

The half-naked warrior, on the other hand, is full of vigor with very little skill, quite willing to trade blow for blow with the Ogre. In fact, the Ogre seemed to be worse for wear as the Adventurer just shuddered slightly from each blow, a light red mist beginning to rise from his body as he was injured.

"Go," Asin says after a moment, shaking her head. They might as well move on, hoping to find another group. As annoying as it was, today had still been a decent day. Daniel nods, mentally gauging which direction to go from his minimap before walking forwards. There was a pair of small caves down this way that often held the floor Champion.

The pair treks forward in silence, paying attention to both the ground and their surroundings. Asin still has to stop Daniel from walking into a hidden pit, chuffing in humor. At his excuse, she just wrinkles her nose, and Daniel edges around the trap, grumbling quietly to himself. Behind him, Asin smirks, though she knows that her friend is unable to smell the open earth beneath the layer of grass that covers the trap. Humans and their pitiful noses.

As they near the caves, Asin's ears begin to twitch. She moves forward quickly, overtaking Daniel as she scans the ground ahead of them for further traps now that she knows where to go. Soon enough, they spot the Ogre Champion himself and the chest behind him. Standing over eleven feet tall, the Ogre Champion is clad in leather armor and wears a pair of metal gauntlets that cover its arms. As they near, the Champion lets out a roar in challenge, rushing the pair.

Daniel raises his crossbow, firing immediately and sinking the bolt into the creature's torso. The blow does nothing to slow the monster even as Asin runs to the side, charging a knife with Piercing Shot as she runs. Throwing the knife, she immediately follows up with Fan of Knives as she releases another knife, focusing on buying time for Daniel to load and fire his crossbow again. The Ogre Champion refuses to be distracted though, catching the first knife on its gauntlet and ignoring the pair of knives that strike it subsequently as it bears down on Daniel.

When it is within ten feet, it jumps and swings its fist, attempting to crush Daniel. Rather than blocking the monster, Daniel drops and rolls, abandoning his crossbow as he comes to his feet. Quickly equipping his shield and mace Daniel starts circling the monster, searching for an opening even as Asin continues to pelt the creature with knives.

The Champion snarls, ignoring the annoying Catkin and the knives that sprout from its back as it jumps forward again, swinging a looping right fist and then following up almost immediately with a straight left. Daniel ducks the first and then is forced to put both shield and mace together to block the second, stumbling backward from the sheer strength of the blow. Even as he attempts to regain his footing, the Ogre steps forwards and leads again with a left, smashing Daniel's hasty guard into him and sending him sprawling to the ground. As Daniel spits out blood from a cut in his mouth, he struggles up to his feet, eyes sparking with restrained fear.

As the Ogre steps forward, Asin's bolo hits, wrapping around the creature's legs. It jerks the Champion to a halt, forcing it to stumble as small lightning arcs jump between its legs. Asin immediately follows up with a Piercing Shot, the thrown knife plunging into the creature's supporting limb and forcing the Ogre to the ground.

Rolling quickly, Daniel just barely manages to avoid being crushed, the unwashed scent of the Champion crossing to his prone form. Kneeling, Daniel sees the elbow the Ogre is using to prop itself up, and he stands, triggering Perin's Blow to smash the limb downwards into the ground. The blow cracks the elbow, forcing it to bend as it meets the ground and Daniel immediately attacks the arm again with another pair of Skill-aided strikes.

Arm twitching, the Champion lashes out, catching Daniel in the side. The Adventurer twists his body, rolling with the blow as best he can. Woozy on his feet, Daniel is forced to cast a Minor Healing on himself as he patches himself up from the multiple heavy blows he has received.

Rather than allowing the monster the chance to stand, Asin rushes forward while Daniel recovers and ducks in close to the Ogre, plunging knives into the back of the creature's exposed thighs, attempting to hamstring the opponent. White sparks fly, and the Champion forcibly defecates itself as the electricity robs the Champion of its bodily functions. The unexpected attack forces Asin to flinch, assaulted as she is by the sudden noxious and unexpected onslaught. Distracted for a brief moment, she does not notice the leg barreling into her side until it is too late and she crashes into the ground, her arm breaking with the impact.

The crippled Champion struggles to its knees, roaring in defiance as Daniel, fully recovered, rushes it. He ducks under the right jab that comes at him, jumping into the air and triggering a Shield Bash as he slams his shield right into the bridge of the Ogre's nose. As the Ogre grips its shattered nose, Daniel throws his body into the next attack that lands against the monster's temple to end the fight.

Limping over, Asin lets out a low yowl of pain to attract Daniel's attention. He then moves to set her arm before he heals her. She whimpers, feeling bone grate as he adjusts her injured limb before the cool wash of the spell rolls over her inflamed nerves. Still, through the pain, she watches the cave entrance and the mana stone in the chest in case of thieves in red cloaks. Having done what little he can for the moment, Daniel hurries over to pocket their loot before returning to help the Beastkin again.

"Enough for today?" Daniel asks, his mana all used up.

"Yes," Asin nods, slowly limping forward. Her arm felt fragile as it always did after a healing and the bruise on her hip was not fully fixed as yet.

"Here, let me fix that…" Daniel reaches out to extend his Gift, and Asin hisses at him, realizing what he is up to. While she doesn't know what exactly the Gift costs him, she understands that all Gifts had a cost. "Asin…"

"Small. I fine," Asin insists, forcing herself to walk with less of a limp.

"Asin…" Daniel prods her, and she grumbles, looking at him. "We're partners."

"Mana. Later," Asin insists and then pauses, adding. "Monster Gift."

"Umm…"

"Fight monster. Use Gift," Asin tries again.

"Okay," Daniel sighs, walking a few further steps and then stopping. His crossbow! Hurrying back, he gets it and checks it over for damage as he returns to his friend who is rubbing at her side. While he isn't happy with her decision, at least she compromised. And he could too.

As they walk back, they spot the group of Adventurers from before, though they are missing one of their numbers. As they near, they see that the group is tying together a series of ropes and are standing around the now-exposed pit trap.

"Problem?" Daniel asks as he nears them, curious more than anything else.

"Our friend fell down the pit trap, but he's okay," a hammer wielding Adventurer answers for the group. "He was hurrying to get to the Champion and well…"

Asin's ears twitch as she listens to the familiar voice of the half-dressed Adventurer shout at the party to hurry up. Obviously, the fall had done little harm to the hardy Adventurer. Prodding Daniel, she gestures for them to keep walking and Daniel nods, turning away.

"Hey, did you two just come from the Champion?" a female Adventurer asks, her voice high and melodic as she hands her part of the rope over.

"Yes," Daniel answers.

"Damn, just the two of you? And you're barely hurt!" Admiration fills her voice as she eyes the pair. "You guys must be pretty high level."

Daniel shrugs and Asin says nothing, though her tail curls slightly in amusement.

"Shit. Now we've got to tell Omrak that you guys killed the Champion," groans another Adventurer. At this statement, all his friends look crestfallen. While the group contemplates this dire news, the pair head off.

"We could leave him there…" Asin overhears one last suggestion as the pair limp off.

***

That evening, Daniel and Asin are seated in the Spinning Top, sharing a meal after a hard day's work. It was a good haul for their level, and the two were celebrating with a good meal and drink. Staring at their now empty plates, they were contemplating the apple pie on offer, wondering if they could fit another piece.

A noise catches the attention of the pair, seated in the corner as they are. The large, half-dressed man in furs cries out in happiness, striding over and grinning widely. "I have found you!"

Daniel frowns, shifting back in his chair and letting a hand drop to his lap. Asin makes no overt move either though her tail starts waving lazily. While it was unusual, it was not unheard of for Adventurers to seek retribution for kills stolen. As the Adventurer nears them, Daniel is surprised to see how young he is - barely more than sixteen at a guess, his face unlined and still growing, hair a pale yellow. The Adventurer moves fluidly, though his encounters earlier in the day show on his shirtless and muscular torso. Still, the bruising seems to be doing little to slow down the exuberant youngster.

"Yes?" Daniel asks, realizing that the Adventurer tops him by nearly a foot. And he might not even be done growing yet!

"I wanted to meet the two mighty Adventurers who beat the Champion by themselves. Such bravery must be toasted! I am Omrak, son of Losin," the youngster speaks, his voice so loud it is almost a shout. He gestures over the nearest waitress. "Come, serve these heroes a drink. I shall take an ale."

"Noisy!" Asin scolds, rubbing at her ears.

"It is very much so, is it not? This a good tavern!" replies Omrak, his volume not changing. "And who are you, heroes?"

"I'm Daniel, and this is Asin," Daniel answers, gesturing to his companion before continuing. "And she was speaking of you."

"Ah." Pausing, Omrak lowers his voice to a stage whisper, "Is this better?"

Asin rolls her eyes as the waitress comes over with three mugs, one filled with Sabu and the other two ale. Eyeing Asin's drink, Omrak says, "What is that purple mixture?"

"Sabu. It's a traditional Beastkin drink," Daniel replies and glances at the mug before he smiles, relaxing slightly. "Thank you for the drink."

"Not at all. Congratulations on killing the Champion. I see my companions were in error - you heroes are entirely uninjured. You must be truly mighty warriors," Omrak says.

"Uhh… no. We healed up," Daniel replies while Asin returns to scraping her plate clean.

"Yes. Of course, you heroes would be able to afford a great many healing potions. They are extremely expensive here, are they not?" Omrak says again, rubbing at his side. "I, myself, have had to purchase a few."

"We did notice your... particular fighting style," Daniel replies, then seizing on the chance adds. "There was a red mist coming from you while you were fighting?"

"The Battle Rage! It is a Skill for our warriors, but it is not as useful against a single opponent," Omrak clarifies, grinning. "You Southerners do not have its like. It gives one extra strength and deadens the pain of the fight."

"That's pretty nice," Daniel nods, realizing where Omrak must come from. Further to the North, past the Gray Mountains was a deep valley that bisected the land where numerous smaller city states existed. Further North of these city states, a small sea separated their lands from Squalak. The mountainous countries that made up that land were well known for calling those who lived further South of them in less harsh and cold climates Southerners.

"Come, let us toast!" Omrak gestures to their drink and Asin sighs, picking up her drink as Daniel does too. "To Great Heroes. May our names be written in the stars!"

Drinking from their cups, they look at Omrak who stands there grinning at them for long moments. As things grow uncomfortable, Daniel coughs and adds, "Would you care to join us?"

"Yes!" Grabbing a nearby seat, Omrak sits down. "Come, heroes; let us speak of our adventures."

Asin rolls her eyes again but stops when Omrak drops coin on the table as he waves the waitress over. "I require dinner and more drinks for my friends!" Well, perhaps Asin could stay if he was paying. Free drinks were free drinks.

***

A week later, the pair walk into Maxwell's store. It had been a long week, working the seventh level again and again for mana stones but they had finally earned enough to cover the cost of the two B Grade stones they were missing as well as to pay for their living expenses for a few more weeks.

"At last! I thought you two would never be done," Maxwell grumbles, taking the pouch and staring at the stones within. He checks them over carefully, nodding in satisfaction. These stones would be more than enough to power the furnace while he was working on his Masterwork. "Are you getting my venom sacs then?"

"Yes," Daniel answers, smiling slightly. "We're going out in two days."

"Two days!" Maxwell says, his voice rising. "Why are you taking so long?"

"We need maps, equipment, provisions," Daniel says. "We also have our lives to live you know. We've been down in the Dungeon every day since we got back from your trip."

"Still…"

"Two days. If we are lucky, we'll get the sacs easily and be back in a few days. Then it'll finally be done," Daniel says and then continues after a pause. "Can I see the pieces?"

Maxwell shuts his mouth around further protests and sighs, waving Daniel over. Ever since Daniel had arrived back, he had been taking measurements and building out the pieces of armor for Daniel, laying each completed piece at the back. While the pieces were mostly finished, final adjustments would need to be made when Daniel put the pieces on to ensure the armor fit comfortably and allowed a full range of motion. As Daniel's eyes fall on the helmet, he reaches out to gently stroke it before glancing at Max.

"Could I maybe put a deposit on this? I don't really have a helmet…" Daniel asks tentatively. It was outside of their contract after all. Maxwell frowns and then looks at the youngster once more before he shakes his head.

"No." Seeing Daniel's crestfallen face, he holds it up to him. "You can keep it. I trust you. Now, put it on and let me adjust it."

Grinning, Daniel takes the arming cap from Maxwell first and then slides on the helmet. The conical helmet covers most of Daniel's face, leaving only his eyes and his mouth exposed, the lower cheek guards flaring downwards a distance. Asin nods approvingly, lips twitching slightly as Daniel shifts around uncomfortably as Maxwell checks the chin straps and the fit. If Daniel was going to wear a helmet and cut down on his senses, he might as well go all the way.

Pulling the helmet off Daniel's face, Maxwell sets to fixing it immediately. Daniel walks over to his friend, murmuring, "You?"

"No," Asin shakes her head and then taps her ears. "No hear. No smell. No see. Bad. Very bad."

"Mmmm…" Daniel grunts and then shrugs after a moment. It was her choice, though as fighting got fiercer, her ability to dodge all blows would become more and more difficult.

Seeing and smelling his concern, Asin chuckles and taps her temple again, "Enchantment. Protection. Buy soon. Daniel pay me."

Daniel frowns for a moment, piecing together finally that she would buy a protection enchantment instead from the money he owed her. Feeling somewhat more comforted, he absently pats at his wallet. Giving away three-quarters of his earnings constantly and having to earn the mana stones meant that he was living lean these days. Still, a custom suit of armor would be worth it, he could feel it in his bones. As Maxwell calls him over, Daniel hurries to him as Asin, bored, bids them farewell. They had set their meeting time in two days, and she had much to do before then.

***

"So soon," Khy'ra says dejectedly, slowly rotating her spoon around the bowl of soup in front of her. Seated in the Spinning Top that evening, the Elf digests the information that Daniel is about to leave again.

"It'll only be a short while this time!" Daniel answers her hurriedly, squeezing her hand. "And I've got tomorrow off if you can get it…"

Khy'ra flashes Daniel a small smile, unwilling to explain that it was his leaving Karlak soon that brought down the Elf. The experienced Elf and former Adventurer knew that with his new armor, it would only be a few months after that before Daniel was done with the Dungeon and thus this town. "Tomorrow… I have meetings in the morning, but I can take the rest of the day off," she says firmly. If she was to lose him, she might as well enjoy it while she could. It was after all her way.

"That's great! I have to do some shopping anyway for the trip," Daniel says, reaching out to squeeze her hand and smiling. "I also have something I want to show you in my room." Khy'ra laughs and, realizing what he said, Daniel begins to blush. "No, it's a helmet!"

This just makes Khy'ra giggle more, and Daniel just gives up, hanging his head. Elise, drawn over by the sight of a giggling Elf raises an eyebrow.

"Daniel has a helmet he wants to show me. In his room," giggles Khy'ra.

Elise, obviously not finding the joke as funny as the Elf, sniffs and walks away. This does little to ease Khy'ra's giggles, though she does reach out to grab Daniel's hand again and give it a squeeze. Tomorrow would do and as many tomorrows as she could get.

Chapter 15

The Pearly Forest was situated southwest of Karlak and technically was still part of Brad. However, the presence of the Querk Spiders and other monsters made the ownership of the forest more theoretical than fact. Spread over hundreds of kilometers, it included lands in both Brad and the Borderlands where the Orc tribes roamed, unchecked.

Still, as dangerous as living next to the forest was, the easy supply of lumber and monster parts for alchemical solutions drove the growth of small frontier villages and the farms required for sustenance. Eventually, the forest would be clear-cut to such a point that a new fort and village would spring up, and the old one would become just another border village.

It was to one such village that Asin and Daniel had visited before they journeyed into the forest itself. Rather than trek through the wilderness on a wild search for the Querk Spiders and the venom sacs they required, the pair had decided to pay for the information from local hunters. Querk Spiders were dangerous, and while their venom sacs were prized, there was significantly easier game to be hunted. As such, it was easier for these hunters to avoid known lairs which gave Adventurers like Asin and Daniel a chance to purchase maps like the one they were even now perusing.

Head bent over the document, Asin and Daniel murmur softly as they peruse the scratched together map. Unfortunately, none of the Hunters they had spoken to had a mapping proficiency, and the document they held could only be barely considered a map through a very broad definition of the term. Twice already the pair had gotten lost in the forest in their search for the first lair, though at least Daniel's own Skill was allowing him to quickly develop an understanding of the layout of their surroundings in his mind. In time, they would certainly be able to navigate the forest significantly easier.

Ears twitching, Asin steps away from Daniel swiftly, drawing her knife. Turning slowly, her gaze locks to their left and Daniel quickly follows suit after stuffing the map away. Even as he reaches for his mace, a small gray creature bounds forwards on three legs in an attack only to be caught in mid-air by Asin's blade. It drops bonelessly, but behind it come even more monsters.

"Gray Mus," Daniel mutters unconsciously as he squats to get a better angle to hit the small, fast moving rodent-like creatures. As their name implied, the rodents were gray in color, each about a handspan in size with a pair of extremely sharp front teeth. While not dangerous individually, the Gray Mus were aggressive pests that reproduced quickly and were willing to swarm larger prey. Still, attacking two full grown humanoids was unusual.

As Daniel swings at the first Mus that nears him, he is distracted by the loud cracking of a branch further behind the tide of creatures. The targeted Mus does not even stop, fleeing past Daniel as their natural predator in the forest comes barreling after them.

The Tento Gulo darts outwards, its long brown body hugging the ground as vine-like tentacles topped with stingers lash out, one after the other to carry the unlucky Mus to its long, snouted maw. The brown-black monster with its long-lean body and oversized head crunched down on each Mus that entered its mouth, needle-sharp teeth tearing apart its unlucky prey.

Asin, having sent a last dagger into a Mus watches as the unlucky rodent is speared as well and brought to the Gulo's mouth, her blade still lodged in its body.

The Gulo pauses its pursuit, staring at the two Adventurers, tentacles whipping around itself. Daniel stays crouched down, watching the monster as Asin readies a pair of throwing knives. For a few tense moments, both parties stare at one another before the Gulo slowly backs away, drawing its captured prey to its mouth as it does so.

It is only when the creature is finally gone that both Adventurers relax, chuckling at each other. There was little to be gained from fighting the monster - after all, they were not here to gather Gulo parts. Better to keep on task.

***

As they finally near the location of the first Querk Spider, Asin prods Daniel to let her take the lead. Now that they are close, her better awareness and perception of the surroundings were important, especially as Querk Spiders were well known for ambushing their prey.

Asin leads Daniel in a circuitous route, skimming around the uneven earth and stepping on branches when she is able. Daniel follows her movements precisely, keeping an eye out for additional dangers. It is only after ten minutes of such walking that Asin comes to a stop, pointing down to a particular, nondescript spot. This, then, would be the new lair of the Querk Spider.

The Querk Spider lived in burrows in the ground with small doors. Unfortunately, due to their size and deadliness, the Spiders would often move these burrows to new locations as it attempted to 'trick' new prey. They were known to even create false burrows, slowly guiding prey to its real location where it waited, ready to pounce from underneath the ground to bite and inject its venom into its prey. As a precaution, both Adventurers had vials of anti-venom purchased in Karlak from the apothecary, but neither looked forward to using it.

As planned, Daniel slowly edges around the corner of the burrow before setting himself. At his signal, Asin walks forward slowly; her tail curled up underneath her body as she readies herself to jump away. When the Spider attacks, it is so fast that Daniel barely sees it move, the trapdoor pushed upwards as the arachnid rears on its legs to sink its fangs into Asin.

Asin jumps back, the yellow-brown stocky arachnid landing where she was. In size, it is only half of hers, barely three feet long from abdomen to thorax but its strong jaws glisten with venom. Surprise attack failed, the Spider begins to scurry back into the safety of its burrow.

Daniel is moving, however, jumping forwards from the side and lashing out at its abdomen with Perin's Blow. The monster is too fast though, and instead of smashing the creature into the air, he smashes one of six legs. This barely slows the Spider down, and before the Adventurers are able to attack again, it has pulled its trapdoor covering over its burrow. As Daniel reaches over to pull against it, Asin barks out a, "No."

"Ba'al's Vomit," Daniel curses, stepping back and away from the trapdoor. They have no way of knowing if the monster will attack again and the trapdoors were reinforced with the creature's silk. It would be pointless to attempt to shatter it without enchanted weapons. "I'm sorry, Asin. I should have been there faster."

Asin nods jerkily, getting her breathing under control. The Spider was fast. Leading Daniel via a safe route out, the pair move away from the lair. It was unlikely the Spider would come out again today.

***

Daniel huffs as another Spider slides away safely beneath its trapdoor, making the young Adventurer tremble with rage. Forcing himself to calm down slightly, Daniel walks away disconsolately while Asin picks herself off the forest floor, wiping away mud and leaves from her toned buttocks.

"This isn't working," Daniel says, and Asin can only give a short nod. In a day and a half, they had only found three such Spiders and had failed to kill two of the three. Of the third, Daniel's attacks had been so strong that he had accidentally crushed the venom sac.

Exhausted, the pair stares at where the Spider continues to hide. "Let's take a break for now."

Asin can only nod and lets Daniel lead them to a nearby stream where they set-up for lunch. The pair are quiet as they consider their plans, attempting to see what they can do to change their tactics. At this rate, it would take weeks before they could gather those three venom sacs.

***

A day later, the pair crouch down in front of a new Spider's lair. Daniel moves to the side once again, crouching down while Asin gently prods their bait. It had taken them the better part of yesterday and this morning to find their bait, though they had been lucky enough to capture three of the split-horned rabbits at once. Now, one of the rabbits had a rope tied around its body and Asin is prodding it, forcing it to head towards the Spider's trapdoor.

There is no warning as the trapdoor is pushed aside and the Spider lunges, fangs spearing the unlucky rabbit. Poison is pumped into the gray, squirming creature and the rabbit's struggles slowdown. As the Spider begins to skitter backward into its burrow, Asin is hauling on the rope that has been looped around a nearby tree, taking up the slack. The Spider jerks to a halt, half in the hole as Asin strains against the monster.

Before the Spider can release the rabbit and escape their trap, Daniel has rushed forwards. Rather than targeting the Spider this time though, he aims his attack at the trapdoor the Spider still holds with two of its legs. Triggering Perin's Blow, he smashes the trapdoor in the side, ripping it free from the Spider's grip and sending it flying into the distance. Without its trapdoor, the Spider spins to attack Daniel, the rabbit dropped and forgotten.

Daniel catches the attack high on his shield, sinking low and letting his knees absorb the shock before he triggers a Shield Bash, slamming the Spider into the air. As it lands, he takes a careful step to the side and crushes a leg, his mace cracking the spindly, hairy appendage.

Asin is scrambling forwards as well, ducking low so that she can slice at both legs on her side with her knives. She scores cuts against both, damaging the legs but as the creature spins again, she finds herself quickly coated with spider silk that the Querk Spider uses to defend itself, spewed forth from its spinnerets. The silk is sticky and tough, restricting her movements and Asin grunts in pain as she attempts to escape.

Seeing his companion in danger, Daniel lays into the Spider, forcing the monster to pay attention to him as he works on the creature's legs. Staying close, he shoves the creature and bashes its jaw when it attempts to push the young Adventurer aside, forcing the monster to give him its legs. Another leg is crippled and then a third soon after, the monster unable to move as fast anymore. As it scrambles aside, attempting to escape now, Daniel darts around to mash the monster's other legs, leaving the creature chittering in anger.

Smiling grimly, Daniel ducks back to look over to his friend. At first, he coughs and then he finally has to giggle a little. To escape, Asin has had to cut off the affected fur, chopping around the silk where it has stuck itself to her body and her clothing. The random patches of uneven fur and gaping holes around her cloak and shirt make Daniel grin, an action that makes Asin hiss at him in anger and dismay.

Freed, Asin stalks right past Daniel, careful to avoid the remaining silk to attack the monster. Drawn back to the task at hand, Daniel works on crushing the abdomen to put an end to the monster, careful to avoid the head where the glands lie.

The monster dead, Asin proceeds immediately to carefully cut up the monster, working to extract the venom sac without damaging it. She chuffs in anger, shaking the blood from the meat and examining the venom sac before discarding it as damaged, working even slower now to extract the second. This is more successful, and Asin purrs happily, her tail waving absently.

Grinning, Daniel holds out the enchanted storage pouch for Asin who carefully stores the gland in it. Even enchanted, the gland would only be good for seven days, but without it, the entire venom would degrade within a day. Still, Daniel cannot help but grin, spotting the bare spot on her tail where Asin had to rip the silk off.

"That's one," Daniel says, and Asin nods. She would need to be more careful on the next Spider. It wasn't as if she carried that many sets of clothing.

***

"Are you done laughing?" Daniel grimaces, tugging at the silk that binds him down. Two Spiders, one sac and a day later, Daniel is caught in spider silk. His shield is stuck to his body, his legs webbed together and he's lying on the ground, able to roll only a short distance back and forth.

Asin sniggers and shakes her head, wishing for a moment there was a way to mark this moment for all time. Daniel groans and just leans his head back on the ground, exercising his patience.

"Asin!"

***

"That'll be a silver for each," the shopkeeper smiles, pointing to the set of dissolution potions on the counter.

"A silver!" Daniel chokes. "They only cost 20 coppers in Karlak!"

"True, true."

"So, 20 coppers, right?"

"In Karlak. It's a silver each here." The shopkeeper smiles again. "You taking them or not?"

"Aaarrggghh!" Fishing the six silvers out, Daniel snatches up the potions after paying. They had used their initial two potions, and they were already wasting half-a-day traveling back just to get a restock. They could not afford to waste more time.

***

"My... face!" Clawing at the silk that has stuck to his face with one hand, Daniel has to remember not to reach with his other hand when he realizes he is unable to move his first. His assailant, having dodged and sprayed Daniel when he first attacked, scrambles away for the nearest tree, dragging the young Adventurer along the ground. Daniel scrambles for his pouch as he bumps over a root, struggling for breath through the corner of his mouth. Hand closing on the potion, he works the stopper free to pour it over the spider silk.

As the Spider reaches the nearest tree, a blurring blue-wreathed dagger pierces its body. Too aerodynamic to pin the creature, it still makes the Spider jerk, slowing its forward momentum long enough for Daniel to pour the potion over the silk. It immediately begins to dissolve as Daniel struggles with the web and breathing.

Asin does not stop, tossing knife after knife at the Spider. Angered, the Spider spins around and attacks Daniel, the long chelicerae in its head shutting on either side of the Adventurer's leg. Only one fang manages to get around the leather armor on Daniel's leg, sliding past the armor and injecting poison into his body. Even as Asin sinks another knife into its body, and Daniel smashes against it, the Spider does not let go, pumping more and more venom into Daniel. As it dies, Daniel is finally able to tear the last of the silk from his face and use both hands to pull its jaws apart.

Asin scrambles over, handing him a potion to combat the paralysis that rushes through Daniel's body. Shivering, Daniel curls up on his side and vomits half the contents of his stomach up. Once Asin has checked with Daniel that he will be fine, she drags the body away, working on the Spider to locate its venom sacs. She grimaces, finding one crushed and the other only half-full. Putting it aside, she mentally does the math. Today was the fourth day since they first managed to get their first sac. Another day and it would rot, so they either had to get one today or risk not having enough. For a time, she watches Daniel who continues to shiver before she hurries over to check on their bait. Only one last rabbit left before they had to find more live bait.

This was going to be tough.

***

"Last chance." Asin points, holding up both the map and the rabbit. Having gone through the vast majority of the easy to get to lairs, the pair would either have to revisit old lairs or journey deeper if they failed again. Daniel grimaces, nodding, running a hand through his hair and finding it catching on remaining spider silk. Lips twisting, he reaches down to pull out his boot knife to cut the glob of silk out, tossing it aside. Well, at least he did not have to worry about a haircut anytime soon.

"Then we better get this right," Daniel growls, rolling his wrist and mace. Days of tramping through the forest, hunting down Spiders that might or might not still be in the locations marked on the map, trapping and dragging live animals and then brief minutes of scrambling, fighting and sometimes, winning, has made the Adventurer short-tempered. So much work for so little gain. No wonder most Adventurers charged such a high rate for these sacs - it wasn't difficult so much as annoying.

Flank, rabbit, charge, and smash. Everything this time works smoothly; the Spider is caught out and its trapdoor is sent spinning away. Asin ducks in close this time and works on the back leg, one after the other while Daniel works on distracting the Spider. He mostly blocks, attacking only once in a while when he has a clear shot, too wary to lash out aggressively.

The monster crippled, Daniel grins and stretches when Asin hisses. He spins around, his eyes widening as he spots the pack of wolves behind him. They let out a little growl, and Daniel slowly edges around the monster towards Asin who has a pair of daggers held out. The wolves snarl again, slowly pacing forwards as they drive the pair away from the Spider. Neither Adventurer wants to start this fight though - they are outnumbered and tired.

Once they are a distance away, the two look at each other as they slide their backpacks on and begin jogging away. Silence lingers for a time as they put distance between them and the pack before a curse flies out finally.

"Ba'al's vomit!"

Chapter 16

Two and a half weeks later, a pair of tired, dirty Adventurers walk into the city of Karlak. The guards nod in recognition to Daniel as he half-heartedly waves in greeting before paying the entrance fee. The two Adventurers trudge in, Asin's tail hanging low and waving disconsolately as they walk, ears pressed low.

The only time the pair perk up is as they pass by a roadside food vendor, the smell of slowly rotating meat sparking a glimmer of interest. Daniel moves over, purchasing a half-dozen sticks from the lady, before handing the pieces over to Asin who scarfs her food down without a word.

At Maxwell's shop, the armorer is stalking back and forth shouting at his apprentices. When he sees the pair, he opens his mouth to berate them for being so late and then stops, his eyes sweeping over their tired, drawn forms. Asin holds up the bag without a word which Maxwell grabs. She hisses, "One day," before stalking away, a cryptic sentence that takes Maxwell only a moment to puzzle out.

Daniel nods too, waiting for Max to check the contents before he walks off, too tired to explain the delay. The last few weeks had been a hell of bad luck, bad planning, and more bad luck. Having lost the Spider to the wolves, the pair had to discard the first sac. For the next few days, they had struggled to find more Querk Spider lairs. When they had finally collected all three sacs and were hurrying back, Daniel had slipped while crossing a log bridge into the water, spilling both himself and the pouch. By the time they had finally managed to fish the pouch out of the water, all three sacs had been compromised, forcing the pair to begin collecting again.

No surprise then that words had been said, none of which were friendly or nice after the incident. The rest of the quest had been completed in a tense, mostly silent atmosphere. If it had not been for Asin's insistence on carrying the pouch, she would have left immediately upon entering the city. As it was, the pair had agreed to ignore one another's existence for the next three days.

Daniel stumbles into the Spinning Top, waving to Elise. She comes over, grimacing and murmurs to him. He stares at her blankly for a time before he slowly exits, heading to the next inn down the road. Daniel's room had been given up for the week, and because of that, Elise had rented it out. She was now filled up and unable to accommodate him.

Groaning, he flops in his room, staring at the peeling paint and the water-stained ceiling. He exhales, breath flowing out with a huff and then he shuts his eyes, exhaustion finally claiming him. As he falls asleep, a last thought crosses his mind.

"I need a bath."

***

Dawn comes too early, bright morning sunshine sifting through the cracked shutters and waking Daniel. He groans, rolling on his side and slowly stands, making his way downstairs for breakfast. Breakfast is surprisingly decent, the porridge filling and warm and the sides of bacon and mushroom heaven sent. Resolved to start becoming human again, Daniel heads upstairs to get his towel and a change of clothing from his bag. Today would be an errand day, one filled with taking care of the many small tasks that need completing after a couple of weeks in the forest. He had socks to darn, clothing and his body to wash, weapons to properly care for, broken equipment to repurchase and more errands to run. Tonight... Tonight he would see Khy'ra he promises himself.

A couple of days later, the pair meet up at Maxwell's shop. Asin stands at the corner, offering her friend a slight smile with a cocked head. Words were said, and relations had strained, but he was her friend. Was she his still? The returning smile from Daniel and the cup of offered tea answers her questions, and her tail relaxes, turning back to swinging idly. A slight flicker of disappointment runs through Asin, she had hoped for more of Elise's heavenly cooking rather than tea, but tea would do.

Daniel does not notice, his attention caught by the 'Closed' sign. As they rap on the door, there is silence for minutes. A second knock brings a harried apprentice to open the door, only for it to be shut again with a whispered the only excuse, "Not now!"

As Daniel raises his hand again, the bar is dropped with a finality, leaving the pair to stand in the early morning chill. Daniel grimaces, staring at Asin who returns his look before she shrugs. Well… Not now then.

***

"This is… nice," Daniel says as he bends down, picking up the mana stone from the Ogre. Asin nods firmly, stretching herself out as they stare around the grassy plains of the seventh floor. It was nice to be back on the seventh floor.

Questing had been necessary, even important. They had learned more of the world, fought in a new dungeon, met new Adventurers and would eventually get Daniel his first full set of custom armor. It had been important, but the Dungeon was much less frustrating. Even the sixth floor and the caverns seemed nostalgic now, difficult but at least they were always progressing. Questing was important, but for now, Daniel was happy to be a real Adventurer, delving into dungeons and facing the monsters that Ba'al would release on the world if it could.

"Next?" Daniel points with his mace before letting it rest on his shoulder, eyes crinkling in humor as Asin finishes stretching and nods. She absently scratches at a bare spot; fur ripped off from the fight. Catching his gaze, she sends him a mild glare before giving up and sticking out her tongue at him before she scampers ahead. Even the loss of her fur would not make her sad today - they were back, doing what they should be doing.

***

It is three days later when the pair finally finds the door to Maxwell's workshop open. Inside, only a single tired apprentice sits at the counter, barely able to keep his head from drooping. Spotting the pair, he gestures them deeper into the shop to the actual smithy portion without getting up from his seat. It was painful being at the bottom of the ladder the apprentice thought to himself as he forced a smile for the next customer.

Behind, Daniel is practically bouncing forwards. He stops when he spots Max who is holding a breastplate to his chest, stroking it gently and buffing the silver inlaid runes. Even to their untrained eyes, the pair can see the difference and care in craftsmanship between the work before them and their own gear. After a time in which Max continues to be oblivious to the pair, Daniel clears his throat.

"Oh, it's you, boy!" Max says as he looks up, eyes deep set and red rimmed. He sets the breastplate down reverently, waving Daniel to the side. "Right, let's get you fitted."

A few minutes later, Daniel is fully outfitted in his armor and forced to do a series of calisthenics. Max asks questions, checking on fit throughout the process though occasionally Daniel has to clear his throat to bring the armorer's attention back to him. After having dressed and undressed a number of times, Max is finally happy with the fit. "Good… good. That's it."

Daniel nods slowly, rotating his hips and torso and then gently bouncing up and down. He grins, the armor barely making any noise, so well was it fitted. He nods firmly to Max, offering his hand. "Thank you!"

"You're welcome," Max shakes his hand and then glances to the side where the enchanted bracers lie. "You know, I could buy those off you and resell them for you. I won't even take a commission."

Daniel opens his mouth and then shuts it, staring at his first ever magical item. He reaches out, letting armored fingers glide across them before he slowly nods. That was the life of an Adventurer, wasn't it? Taking what was useful, discarding what was not. He wanted, no, he needed to progress.

Max calls out without hesitation to his apprentice, making the youngster take the bracers away for cleaning. Obviously, a little work needed to be done before he would dare show that work in his store!

Turning to Asin, he grins at her. "I have a little something for you too." Reaching behind, he pulls out a small, thin metal gorget with a separate plate piece that hangs down the front which he hands to her. It is not wide at all and curves slightly down in the front and back to allow greater movement. As Asin takes it, her eyes widen at how light the piece is. Seeing her reaction, Max smirks. "I had some extra steel."

Asin takes the piece, quickly buckling it on and adjusting the leather straps to ensure it sits properly. Max looks it over and nods after a moment, more than pleased with the fit. As Asin fingers the collar, wondering at the cost of getting such a piece enchanted by Tharuk, she can only add, "Thank you."

"You're welcome." He smiles again, his hand unconsciously resting on the breastplate next to him. "Now, get out!"

The pair quickly exits, understanding how mercurial Max could get, especially after spending the last few days with little rest. A shared glance is all the pair need before they begin to trot quickly to the Dungeon. Time to try out their new toys!

***

"Let's go, big boy!" Grinning, Daniel hefts his shield and mace as he runs forward. They had been extremely lucky, having literally stumbled upon the Ogre Champion a bare two hours after making their way down to the seventh level. Chest and Champion in their sight, the pair immediately charge the creature before them.

Daniel skids to a stop just outside of the Ogre Champion's range, dodging the blow that swings down in front of him and digs a divot into the ground. Behind, Asin throws a series of knives that multiply, cutting into the Champion and distracting it. Daniel darts in immediately to the left, swinging his mace into the creature's side and feeling a bone crack as Perin's Blow catches it.

However, even as the monster is lifted off the ground, it backhands Daniel, the club smashing into the Adventurer's side.

The club cracks into his body hard, throwing him off his feet and forcing Daniel to work to recover his balance. He grins, elation running through him as he realizes that he is barely hurt - that blow itself should have seriously bruised, if not broken his ribs. More confident than ever now, Daniel darts back in as Asin throws another knife filled with blue energy, the Piercing Shot drilling into the Ogre's eye.

As the creature rears back in pain, clutching at its ruined orb, Daniel crashes into the monster with his shield, triggering a Shield Bash into its short ribs. The monster leans over, allowing Daniel to lash out with a pair of Skill enhanced blows even as Asin closes and hamstrings the Champion. Crashing to the ground, crippled and in pain, the monster is quickly dispatched.

Asin and Daniel stare at the blue lights as they slowly dissipate, shaking their heads in amusement. It seemed strange that such a simple change would make such a difference, but with less concern about getting hurt, Daniel found himself being more aggressive. This took the pressure off Asin who was then able to focus on dealing damage and distracting the Champion. It was a knock-on effect that made it possible for what was a difficult fight before to become so much simpler.

On retrieving her knives, Asin moves to pick up the mana stones before getting a confirming nod from Daniel. Time to head for the eighth floor then.

***

Three hours later, Daniel pants as he stands above the pair of fallen Ogre corpses. The eighth floor had much the same geography as the seventh - wide open lands with glowing blue cavern walls. However, the Ogres came in pairs at least and sometimes as many as four at a time. Fights were more difficult as the Ogres often grouped up, attacking Daniel in a desperate attempt to overwhelm him. Often, Daniel would be forced to stay on the defensive, pulling the monsters with him while Asin finished one, relieving the pressure sufficiently for Daniel to fight back.

Rotating his shoulder, he forces his breathing to slow down, trying to calm down his heart. This last group had managed to take his feet off him, and he had spent a good few minutes curled up, being beaten on by the enormous monsters. His new armor and careful positioning had allowed him to survive, though he ached all across his body. Rubbing at a bruise on his face, he focuses on casting a Minor Heal, his body stitching itself together, as Asin finishes collecting the stones. Healed, he finally pays attention to his new notification.

Level Up!
Adventurer Level 7
You have gained 5 attribute points

Finally! He had managed to get past the level he had lost and was finally climbing again. He might not reach Level 10 before the end of the Dungeon, but at the least, he was on the way. There was a lot of work left, and he certainly felt that they needed to spend more time working this level, but soon, soon, they'd be done!

Name: Daniel Chai
Class: Level 7 Adventurer (0%)
Sub-classes: Level 7 (Miner) (14%)
Human (Male)

Statistics
Life: 243
Stamina: 243
Mana: 177

Attributes
Strength: 23
Agility: 21
Constitution: 29
Intelligence: 18
Willpower: 18
Luck: 14

Skills
Unarmed Combat: Level 3 (38/100)
Clubs: Level 9 (74/100)
Archery: Level 2 (48/100_
Shield: Level 8 (24/100)
Dodge: Level 6 (09/100)

Combat Sense: Level 6 (17/100)
Perception: Level 6 (27/100)
Mining: Level 7 (78/100)
Healing: Level 8 (98/100)
Herb Lore: Level 3 (31/100)
Stealth: Level 2 (14/100)
Cooking: Level 3 (29/100)
Singing: Level 2 (14/100)

Skill Proficiencies
Double Strike
Shield Bash
Perin's Blow
Mapping (II)

Spells
Minor Healing (I)

Gifts
Martyr's Touch - The caster may heal oneself or others by touch and concentration, sacrificing a portion of his life to do so. Cost varies depending on the extent of the injuries healed.

Chapter 17

Learning magic was strange, especially when one's previous experience with learning magic was through a Skill Up mused Daniel. Seated across Khy'ra's dining table this evening, the black-haired Adventurer watches as she weaves the spell slowly again, eyes squinted to catch each change in formula and mana flow. As she finishes the spell, she lets the magic disperse and slumps backward, rubbing her temples.

There were three portions to learning any magical spell. First, came the knowledge of the subject matter - a requirement to understand how the magic interacted with the substance or individual it affected. It was why more Advanced Spells were locked till one gained a greater level of the underlying skill. Second, came the spell formula which was a combination of alchemical formula, a way of thinking and a method of mana weaving all combined. Lastly, came personal flair - the way a student learned to apply the first and second portions of knowledge in their own understanding of mana. Of course, as every teacher had their personal flair, the process of studying a spell required a student not only learn the spell but learn how their master cast it and how to strip out the portions that did not work with their particular understanding and ability with mana.

A common saying was that magic users spent as many years searching for a teacher as they did learning magic itself and why teachers were particularly picky about students. A bad match between teacher and student could result in months if not years of wasted effort by both parties.

Unfortunately, Daniel neither had the time nor money to find a suitable instructor. He only had one particularly generous, beautiful elf that was willing to spend date night at home, casting and recasting a spell again and again so that he could attempt to learn it. Focusing, Daniel tried again, slowly pushing the mana out as he recalled the arcane formula.

"Yes… no, too much, just a little…" Khy'ra whispers encouragement along as they work together.

An hour later, Daniel is done as his mana is drained. Khy'ra smiles, pushing him back in his seat and plopping onto his lap. "Good! Very good."

"Ughh… I barely got past the first sequence," Daniel mutters as he wraps his arms around her body, squeezing it gently and nuzzling her neck.

"It was our first lesson," the Elf points out and then leans down, letting his breath tickle her ear. "You'll do better the next time. Just keep practicing."

Daniel nods, already distracted by the squishy, pleasant presence on his lap. He takes her ear into his mouth, nibbling on the lobe as Khy'ra catches her breath, squirming slightly. There were certain advantages to this kind of lessons for sure.

***

"Asin," Khy'ra calls out in horror, rushing forward to grab the young Catkin's arms. "What happened?"

Asin begins to growl and purr, answering Khy'ra in Catkin while Daniel stands stupefied, wondering what the fuss is about. As Khy'ra strokes one of Asin's arms and the patch of bare fur before pointing to another, realization slowly arrives. The pair continues to converse in Catkin, growling and purring at each other as they start walking off, leaving Daniel to follow after. His attempts at learning Catkin had been abject failures, his ear unable to locate the differences in words well enough for him to even begin learning thus far.

Resolving to follow along without complaining, Daniel perks up slightly halfway through their walk, the group having left the city a while ago. Khy'ra's not-so-covert glance and quick grin is enough to let him know that he is the object of conversation, though neither lady seems inclined to enlighten him further. Left alone, Daniel can only brood about what they might be discussing about him for the rest of their walk.

"Tharuk!" Khy'ra calls out to her friend, waiting for the Dwarf to exit his workshop before waving to him. Hours of walking has the group finally arriving at the lonesome building that makes up the Dwarf's workshop and home. "I brought visitors."

Tharuk laughs out loud and waves to the Elf, nodding in greeting to both Asin and Daniel. Asin bows slightly while Daniel waves, both sniffing the air as they smell lunch on the stove.

"Aye, lass. I remember. Lunch is nearly ready," Tharuk replies and waves them in, returning to his kitchen while the group takes seats around his cluttered kitchen cum workshop table. Asin's nose twitches, mentally cataloging the spices that are being used – Bloor, cinnamon, cardamom, Hunik salt, duck fat.

Seated together, Daniel whispers to Khy'ra, "What were you talking about?"

"Girl stuff," Khy'ra says.

"You were laughing!"

"We were," Khy'ra replies and refuses to say more.

"Right, lunch! Grab your plates, you lazy lot!" Tharuk cries out from the kitchen, drawing the attention of the group. Lunch is a pleasant, tasty and filling stew that is rapidly consumed with the freshly baked bread Tharuk pulls from the oven. It is only as they near the end does Tharuk bring the conversation back to the reason they came. "So, I hear one of you has a commission for me?"

Asin nods, holding up the steel gorget for Tharuk. "Shield."

Tharuk raises an eyebrow, picking up the gorget and looking it over. He hums and haws as he tests the piece, squinting and brushing fingers across it before slowly nodding. "Good work. Master-level crafting and materials. I can work with this for sure. A Shield Enchantment is costly though, more than most."

Asin nods. "Have coin."

Tharuk raises a slight eyebrow before he gently places the gorget down and begins to stroke his beard, staring at Asin, "Well, since you're a friend of Khy'ra, I can do it for fifteen Gold."

Daniel coughs, his eyes wide and Khy'ra sighs, grabbing his hand and standing up. "We'll just leave you two then."

Asin just nods, continuing to stare at Tharuk as she hisses, "Four."

"Four! I'd have to sell my house at Four! Eleven," Tharuk says and then in the silence as Asin stares at him, gestures to the side. "Pie?"

As Daniel is dragged out by Khy'ra, Daniel plaintively cries, "I wanted some pie too."

***

"The Dungeon is closed!" a voice shouts into the Top where Daniel has finally managed to get a room again. Seated in the dining room with Asin and Khy'ra for dinner later that evening, the shout catches everyone's attention.

"What?"

"No…"

"That's not possible!"

"What did he say?"

"QUIET!" shouts Elise as she strides over to the street youth who has brought the news. She prods him in the chest, getting him to repeat his message. When he is done, he is already running to the next inn after getting a tip from Elise. She turns to everyone who is waiting. "The Dungeon doors are closed. Adventurers can exit, but no one can enter. There is a lot of noise coming from the Dungeon too, grinding and screeching."

A hush falls over the inn, many Adventurers looking at one another in search for an answer. Eventually, all eyes fall on Khy'ra, waiting for the wise and long-lived Elf to speak. She smiles at everyone, waving slightly before she speaks, her mild voice carrying. "It's changing its configuration. It sometimes happens with Dungeons, though it's rare. It'll re-open."

The Adventurers, guards, and other patrons relax slightly.

Ken calls back with a question. "How long?"

"I don't know. It's variable. Maybe a day, maybe a week, maybe a few months." Khy'ra shrugs before adding, "It depends on how much is changing. The longer it's closed, the more it will have changed."

This statement makes a few Adventurers shift uncomfortably. Many made their daily living working the second sector of the floor, breaking down crawler walls and collecting crawler sacs for a living. It was good money that held little risk for these experienced Adventurers and a change in the Dungeon could mean a loss of their livelihood.

Daniel and Asin exchange worried glances. Their journeys and the needs of the quest had driven them to rely on their savings more than they had liked. It was only in the last few weeks that they had begun to replace their spent coin. A long break could be difficult for both of them. Without a word, they both stand and head for the door,

Daniel snatching a quick kiss with Khy'ra first as she gets crowded by other Adventurers.

Best see what quests were available before they were all snatched up.

***

"Omrak?" Daniel frowns, walking over to the big warrior who is standing disconsolately by the Quest board in the Adventurer's Guild. A week after the closing of the Dungeon, the board was now bare as Adventurers scrambled to get what little jobs there were to fill their coin purse. Sadly, few Adventurers had much in savings - their lifestyles rarely predicated long-term plans.

At his name, the young Adventurer turns, flashing a strained smile at Daniel and Asin, "Morning, heroes!"

"Where's your party?" Daniel asks as he looks around and Omrak's face falls again.

"Gone," he mutters and then straightens his broad shoulders. "They have left for Peel."

"Split?" Asin clarifies and Omrak nods slightly, his face tired.

At Daniel's frown, Omrak adds, "My party, they felt I was fighting too recklessly. Using too many health potions."

A memory of the laughing warrior, standing and trading blows with Ogres flash through both Adventurer's minds. "Why don't you wear armor?"

"I have no coin," Omrak grimaces, his gaze lingering longingly on Daniel's leather armor that he wears today. "It is impossible. I fight as hard as I can, and no matter what level I go to, I can never earn enough!"

Daniel opens his mouth and then shuts it, unsure of what to say. Asin offers a slight, toothy smile before she waves goodbye. As there are no jobs again this morning, she has other duties to attend to. Daniel nods goodbye to his friend as Omrak continues to stare at the board. "Well, I guess I should get to work."

"Work?" Omrak says.

"I'm at the Clinic for now," Daniel replies and then eyeing Omrak he adds. "You know, I heard that Levi near the docks is always looking for strong dock workers to help unload the barges."

"Thank you! I will speak with this Levi. It is not the work of heroes, but even heroes must eat." Without waiting further Omrak dashes out, a wide grin on his face. Daniel just looks at the disappearing form of the large Northerner, somewhat bemused. Well, he had best get to work too.

***

The distant cry of a newborn baby and the creaking of old wood are the only noises that break the silence of the night. Seated at Khy'ra's kitchen table, Daniel nurses a cup of tea in the dark, staring unseeing into her kitchen. Sleep has eluded him again tonight, his thoughts unwilling to still even as he lay in bed with his girlfriend.

He had been putting off the decision for weeks now, the pressing question of whether to join a guild. At first, he had delayed it till he had completed his quest. Then, he had delayed it to 'test' his new armor. Then, he had made excuses that he was learning a new spell for free with Khy'ra. During the day, when he worked at the Clinic, these excuses made perfect sense. However, late at night, with no Dungeon in the city nor work to keep his mind busy, his excuses felt like what they were, excuses.

He was delaying making a decision, procrastinating, because he did not want to make one. He knew, truly knew, that he had no desire to be a Questor, solely living on the returns of quests like others. Nor did he wish to be a Lifer, working a section of Dungeon over and over again like a, like a Farmer. Both those decisions were easy.

Joining a guild though, becoming part of something larger, that was more difficult. He could not casually dismiss that opportunity. Guilds would allow him to grow, to become stronger faster. He would not need to rely on his girlfriend, would not have to scramble and scrabble for coin to develop his arms and armor. He would have more party members, more training, more opportunities.

And yet… And yet.

"Daniel?" Khy'ra walks into the room, pulling her robe closed as she turns to his moonlight-silhouetted form. Seeing her, an involuntary smile crosses Daniel's face, his face lightening. He holds a hand out, and she takes it, sliding onto his legs with ease as he hugs her to him. She bends down, trading a kiss before she murmurs, "Problems?"

"Just… thinking," Daniel answers and hugs her again, resting his head on her shoulder. Khy'ra nods slightly, staying quiet till Daniel breaks the silence himself. "I was thinking about the guilds again."

"Oh," her reply is soft as Khy'ra struggles to keep her tone neutral. She knew this day had to come, but still…

"I just, it makes sense you know?" he says plaintively. "There's so much to gain from it. I'm doing okay right now, doing good, but… it makes sense!"

"Mmmhmmm," Khy'ra replies, biting her lip in the dark to not add anything.

"I just…" He hugs her again, staring into the dark. "I wanted to be an Adventurer ever since I was a kid you know. I heard all the stories, remembered all the names. Going into the deepest Dungeons, fighting the hardest monsters, being the best and keeping everyone safe. It was what heroes did.

"And I can do that. I have to do that with a guild. No hero ever grows without a guild, a strong party beside him. I know that. But…" Daniel shakes his head, whispering the last. "I don't want to go."

"Because you're scared?" Khy'ra turns, meeting Daniel's eyes at last. "Or because you're comfortable?"

"I'm… happy," Daniel answers her after some thought, his lips twisting crookedly. "I'm happy, learning with you and Asin. Fighting my way through slowly. I hate questing, but even then, when we are done, it's so satisfying."

"Then that's your answer," Khy'ra says.

"But…"

"Daniel. A word of advice from an old… Adventurer," Khy'ra says, smiling slightly. "When you look back at your life, it's not the stories that you remember. Or the Dungeons you visit or the monsters you vanquish. It's your friends and your struggles. You have time. Time to join a guild. Time to get better. I know it doesn't seem like that, but you do have time. Enjoy it while you can."

Slowly nodding, Daniel leans against her. A small part of him still wonders if this is the right choice, but… he was happy. Was that not what everyone truly wanted? Even if he had to leave, perhaps he could be happy here for a little longer.

***

Bursting through his clinic door, the messenger pant as he catches his breath before he announces his news, "It's open!"

Daniel opens his mouth and then shuts it, his eyes lighting up with excitement. He glances at his latest patient and then casts Minor Healing, the open cut on her hand stitching close as Daniel grins, grabbing his cloak from the coat hanger. As he hurries out, he looks to the receptionist who laughs, waving Daniel away. She understands she cannot stop him. After all, everyone here was a volunteer.

As he runs along, Daniel finds himself joining a stream of other interested parties. He notices other Adventurers, of course, on-sight, but there are numerous other citizens who hurry along. Nearly three weeks of having the town's biggest income earner being shut down has hurt the livelihood of many, and so, the interest is not unexpected.

As Daniel finally reaches the town square, he finds it already crowded. He growls slightly, unable to press forward or see anything. After a while, hushing noises are made, and the crowd slowly falls silent as the Guard Captain stands, shouting.

"The Dungeon is open. No one has been allowed in as yet. All Adventuring parties are to visit the Adventurer's Guild to receive their entry number. Entry will be gated from tomorrow onwards. Now go home!"

As the word gets passed down, other guards start taking up the call, directing the crowd out of the town square. Questions are rebuffed, and slowly Daniel manages to make his way to the Guild Hall. As he nears, he spots a familiar figure crouched on top of a statue, licking the fur on her hand.

"Asin!"

The Catkin stares and then waves, dropping down to meet him. Her grin widens as she meets Daniel's excited gaze. The Dungeon was open!

###

Author's Note

If you enjoyed reading the book, please do leave a review and rating. Not only is it a big ego boost, it also helps sales and convinces me to write more in the series!

If you enjoyed this, check out my other series:
- Life in the North (An Apocalyptic LitRPG)
https://readerlinks.com/l/729295
- A Gamer's Wish (An Urban Fantasy LitRPG)
https://readerlinks.com/l/729151
- A Thousand Li (a cultivation series inspired by Chinese wuxia and xianxia novels)
https://readerlinks.com/l/729231

For more great information about LitRPG series, check out the Facebook groups:
- Gamelit Society
https://www.facebook.com/groups/LitRPGsociety/
- LitRPG Books
https://www.facebook.com/groups/LitRPG.books/

About the Author

Tao Wong is an avid fantasy and sci-fi reader who spends his time working and writing in the North of Canada. He's spent way too many years doing martial arts of many forms and having broken himself too often, now spends his time writing about fantasy worlds.

If you'd like to support him directly, Tao now has a Patreon page where previews of all his new books can be found!

- https://www.patreon.com/taowong

For updates on the series and the author's other books (and special one-shot stories), please visit his website: http://www.mylifemytao.com

Subscribers to Tao's mailing list will receive exclusive access to short stories in the Thousand Li and System Apocalypse universes: https://www.subscribepage.com/taowong

Or visit his Facebook Page: https://www.facebook.com/taowongauthor

About the Publisher

Starlit Publishing is wholly owned and operated by Tao Wong. It is a science fiction and fantasy publisher focused on the LitRPG & cultivation genres. Their focus is on promoting new, upcoming authors in the genre whose writing challenges the existing stereotypes while giving a rip-roaring good read.

For more information on Starlit Publishing, visit our website!
https://www.starlitpublishing.com/

You can also join Starlit Publishing's mailing list to learn of new, exciting authors and book releases.
https://starlitpublishing.com/newsletter-signup/

Read an excerpt of Book 3 of Adventures on Brad series:
A Dungeon's Soul

Chapter 1

Dawn light filtered through the wooden shutters of Daniel Chai's room in the Spinning Top. He shivered, pulling his blankets closer to his body for a moment as the late autumn morning chill made itself known to him. Long years of discipline forced him to sit up now that he was awake. He ran a hand through his hair, smiling slightly at the uneven cut that Khy'ra, his girlfriend, had given him. She was a dangerous Adventurer, a beautiful Elf, and a kindly Healer, but the one thing she was not was a decent barber.

After stretching slowly to his full five foot eight inches, Daniel walked to the windows after wiping himself down, sliding a shirt back on. He threw the shutters open and looked out at the sprawling city of wood and stone before him, then leaned outwards slightly as he stared at the center of town to spot the Dungeon entrance and the Adventurers' Guild. Early as it was, he could see streams of Adventurers entering and exiting the Dungeon, traversing the pathway between Guild and Dungeon to sell their loot before resting.

The Karlak Dungeon had reopened in the last few days after being closed for weeks as the Dungeon reconfigured itself. The wave of relief that had risen through the city when it was made clear that it was still a Beginner Dungeon had been palatable. As every Adventurer had to start again from the first Level, the Adventurers' Guild had instituted a lottery system to stagger entry. Eventually, the more experienced Adventurers would trickle down to the lower levels and entry would no longer need to be staggered, as the Adventurers would all be spread out across its many levels. Eventually.

Daniel sighed again, pulled his head back in, and finished dressing. Unfortunately, their party had drawn a slot for tomorrow, leaving them to wait another day. Weeks without their most important income source meant that he needed to work whatever jobs he could find on the quest board if he wanted to eat tomorrow. Staying in bed was not an option.

Walking down the stairs, he waved to Elise, the Spinning Top's owner, who was delivering food to the floor. The matronly blonde smiled at Daniel, nodding to a free table while she delivered watered-down beer, wine, and a mix of eggs, bacon, and leafy greens to the table. Daniel idly noted that the plates were nearly overflowing with greens as the very last harvest had been pulled from the ground. Soon, only canned vegetables and a small variety of magically preserved vegetables would be available.

"Morning, Elise," Daniel greeted the innkeeper as she arrived with his breakfast. Elise just flashed him a smile, too busy to chat while he dug into the meal with gusto. As he finished up,

Elise dropped off a pair of wrapped lunches at his table.

Outside, having retrieved his leather armor, shield, and mace, Daniel quickly joined the flow of humanity as he headed to the Guild. Daniel casually eyed the crowds who were mostly made up of human townsfolk with the occasional glimpse of a Beastkin. Early as it was, most Adventurers were either already in the Dungeon or still asleep. Once he arrived at the Adventurers' Guild, he found his partner, Asin, waiting for him.

"Morning, Asin," he greeted his friend and fellow party member. The smaller Catkin was crouched on the stairs that led up to the building, licking at her paw while her tail lazily waved in the air behind her. Jade eyes glinted in amusement as Daniel handed her the packet of food, which she quickly slipped into her bag, ensuring it was strapped in and out of the way of her additional throwing knives.

"Daniel," Asin purred. The Catkin as always kept her speaking to the minimum, being one of the unlucky few who found it painful to speak in the human tongue of Brad. Unfortunately, as hard as Daniel worked at it, he found it difficult to shape his throat and tongue to speak the common Beastkin language.

"Checked out the quest board yet?" Daniel asked as he walked up the stairs. Asin stood smoothly, her movements all feline grace. At the shake of Asin's head, Daniel nodded contentedly. Inside, the Adventurers' Guild buzzed as Adventuring parties cashed out Mana Stones, hung out regaling each other with tales of the new floors, and generally made a mess. Asin's ears perked up as she swiveled her head from side to side, listening in on the conversation. Being the third day of the Dungeon opening, talk mostly centered around the first floor and as such, Asin learnt nothing new.

The quest board was literally a pair of rolling wooden boards upon which the attendants at the Guild posted new requests. The board itself was separated into three portions depicting the most common quest types—Delivery, Collection, and Miscellaneous. Unlike the previous few weeks, the board was not stripped bare of all quests as more and more Adventurers went back to the Dungeon to earn coin.

Lips pursed, Daniel slowly read through the posted offers. Unlike many of his peers, the former Miner had been taught to read, so he ignored the symbols posted on the bottom right for the illiterate, instead studying the board for a suitable option.

"Ah, brave heroes! The morning's fire greets you all!" The roared greeting makes Asin wince. Everyone in the Guild briefly turned to view the youthful barbarian who was the cause of the ruckus. Standing nearly a foot taller than Daniel, the blond-haired, tunic-clad muscular Northerner towered over the Adventurers within, a friendly smile on his face as he walked in. Carrying only a single, large sword, the barbarian strode over to the quest board, his grin widening as he spotted Asin and Daniel.

"Morning, Omrak," Daniel greeted the youngster, shuffling over slightly to give the barbarian space.

"This? Is this quest worthy of a hero?" A brief few seconds later, Omrak was pointing out a quest with a meaty finger.

"Uhhh ..." Daniel read the quest notice, lips twitching. "That's a request for beaters for the upcoming Fall Hunt. It's a few days away and you'd need to make your way there. Not bad pay though."

"Ah ..." Omrak rumbled, staring at the quest. Daniel raised an eyebrow and Omrak shrugged as he answered the unspoken question. "I have no party. I must wait a few more days before entering the Dungeon. This quest work, it is less than heroic but better than the docks."

"No luck with finding a party so far?" Daniel asked.

"No. I fear I must wait for a new group or grow strong myself," Omrak said, clapping a hand to his chest.

"Well, we're going in tomorrow ..." Daniel began to say before he was elbowed in the side by Asin. She snarled at him, making him blink.

"Hero Asin ...?"

"Later," Asin growled as she dragged Daniel to a nearby booth. She lowered her voice then, snarling at him. "No offer."

"But why?" asked Daniel. "It won't be for long and he needs some help."

"First floor. Lousy stones. Split three way," Asin said, her tail lashing out behind her.

"Uhh …" Daniel quickly parsed the sentences together before he blinked. "You don't want to help Omrak because we won't earn enough?"

Asin nodded firmly, making Daniel grimace.

"He's not earning a lot right now. It won't hurt for him to join us and we could use his help at lower levels. He's roughly on the same level as we are so he wouldn't be holding us back," Daniel said quickly, lining up his arguments.

"Expensive," Asin repeated.

"Yeah, but he can carry more than we can."

Asin paused, clearly taken by that thought. Pressing his advantage, Daniel continued, "You know you can't carry much and neither can I. With more help, we could potentially clear the second floor in a single day."

Asin frowned before she finally answered, "Third."

"That's …"

"Third."

"Fine!" Daniel grimaced, knowing that pushing to do three floors in a single run was going to be difficult. However, the Guild had agreed that any party that managed to make it to the third floor would be eligible to enter the Dungeon at any time. Having won her way, Asin stalked back to the big barbarian who had been watching the argument with interest.

"Join. Carry. Go fast," Asin hissed at the big man, holding her fingers up as she spoke. "Equal share."

Omrak grinned, clapping the diminutive Catkin on the shoulder and staggering her. "Thank you, hero! You shall not find fault in our progress. I shall be your shield, your sword, and your back!"

"Loud!" Asin complained to Daniel as she grabbed a quest off the board and stalked off to join the line awaiting an attendant.

"Omrak, quieter, please," Daniel said, grinning slightly at his Catkin friend, who was rubbing her shoulder discretely.

"Of course, hero!" Omrak said in a stage whisper.

"Tomorrow, at the entrance. Dawn."

"I shall be there. But for now, I must meet with the Master of Docks. I shall avail myself to the boats one last day."

"Yeah, you do that. See you, Omrak." Having said his goodbyes, Daniel strode over to his waiting friend, who held the quest notice out for Daniel to read. He winced as he read it over, grumbling. "Really?"

"Good coin."

"I know …" Daniel sighed again and slipped the quest notice into his pouch. Well, he was asking her to help.

***

Hours later, Daniel stifled a slight groan as he hauled the next basket of fish up the steep hill. As Omrak would have said—this was not a hero's work. However, it was decent-paying work for both of them—at least, so long as the fish were swimming. It was the last week of the run and the Fishermen's Guild had finally opened up fishing on the river, ensuring that the nets and fishing traps were running full-bore. Even if Adventurers were not the preferred day laborers, this week any extra pair of hands was gratefully taken.

Daniel just wished that he was not stuck doing the heavy labor. Unfortunately, like most of the hired Adventurers, he had no Skills or background in crafting, so fixing the nets or the traps was out. His only saving grace here was his strength and endurance, and so he found himself trudging up the hill with baskets filled with fish. In the river, Asin—with her natural grace and her superb aim—was having the time of her life with the nets. Even without a Skill related to fishing, she was pulling a significant number of fish out.

As he came back down the hill, Daniel watched Asin tromp out of the freezing water to warm up against the nearby braziers. Enchanted galoshes kept her feet and thighs warm but did nothing for her torso. Daniel had to hide a smile when she finally exited and shook herself hard, sending droplets of cold water cascading from her fur. A choked snort from behind him told Daniel that he was not the only one to find the wet Catkin amusing.

If he had to spend a day outside of the Dungeon, this was not a bad way to do so. Still, as Daniel stretched and looked up into the sky, he could not help but look forward to the next day.

***

"Daniel," Khy'ra greeted him as she entered her house. "I got your message at the Clinic."

"Khy'ra." He bent forwards, planting a quick kiss on her lips before he turned back to frying the fish. One good thing about working the river today—dinner was easily served. "Everything good at the Clinic?"

"The usual." Khy'ra shrugged. "Nothing that needs your Gift, though if you could spare a few minutes later, we have a few patients that could use a Healing."

Daniel nodded, relieved that he would not be required to use his Gift. A small number, maybe one in a thousand, were Gifted with an ability upon birth. The usefulness and strength of the ability varied but what never did was that the use of a Gift had a cost. For Daniel, that cost of using his Gift was the loss of a portion of his memories, his experience, his Skills. However, his Gift also provided him an uncanny understanding of the body which allowed him to learn and progress in the use of more traditional Healing magic.

"After dinner," Daniel said.

"Of course. Worked the river today?" Khy'ra asked as she walked up beside him, breathing in the aroma of the fried fish. She could smell crushed pepper, the pork fat that she had saved, dried thyme, red peppers, and something else. Brows furrowed, the Elf stared at the tantalizing dish.

"Asin's recipe," Daniel answered, prodding the fish once again before taking it out of the frying pan.

"Should I get the milk then?" Khy'ra teased as she walked to set the table.

"I fixed it," Daniel said proudly. Once again, he was grateful that the Catkin was as dedicated to good food as he was—his journeys in the last few months had taught him that this was not the case with most other Adventuring parties. On the other hand, the Beastkin had a tendency to eat intensely spicy foods—something that puzzled Daniel, considering their expanded senses.

"Oh good," Khy'ra said, and Daniel laughed. As much as Khy'ra complained, he could still recall her stuffing her face without complaint the last time Asin was here cooking for them all.

"You're headed into the Dungeon tomorrow?" Khy'ra asked as she finished setting the table, watching as Daniel fished out the bread from the oven. There were many reasons she cared for this young Adventurer, but the way he fed her certainly helped. A touch of sorrow flickered across her face as she recalled that he would be leaving soon. Like most humans, they stepped into and out of her life.

"Yes. Do you recall the Northerner? Omrak?"

"I've seen him around. Big man."

"Uhh …" Daniel paused, noting the admiring tone in her voice before he shook away the flash of jealousy. "Yes. He'll be joining us. At least for a few levels."

"Mmmm … that's good," Khy'ra said around a mouthful of fish.

Daniel blinked, uncertain of whether she was referring to his cooking or Omrak. Seeing his confusion, Khy'ra's eyes crinkled in humor and Daniel realized she had done it on purpose. Seeing him growl playfully at her, the Elf finally relented.

"It's good that you've gotten more help. There are a lot of Dungeons that can't be completed without more members," Khy'ra clarified. Daniel nodded, knowing what she said was true. However, both he and Asin were workaholics, and finding others who were willing to keep up with them would have been difficult. Daniel, however, had a very good feeling about Omrak.

Biting into the fish himself, Daniel turned the conversation to Khy'ra's day, pushing aside thoughts of the Dungeon and Adventuring. They would have more than enough to discuss tomorrow.

Continue reading here:
https://readerlinks.com/l/729199